AMERICAN COWBOYS

First Printing, 2024

ISBN: 9798218377144 (HC)
9798218388188 (PB)
9798218377137 (EPUB)

Library of Congress Control Number:
2024905002

American Cowboys

Aaron C. Rhodes

Rhiannyn Aubree Publishing

I want to dedicate this book to my boys Landyn, Warner and Maverick.

Contents

Preface   **1**

One
El Paso Rescue   3

Two
The Rose Ranch   6

Three
Battle of Tupelo   10

Four
Frank   21

Five
The Clock Tower Church   27

Six
The Baron   34

Seven
Navajo   40

Eight
Barbed Wire Prairie   45

Nine
Red River Railway   50

Ten
The Dance   61

Eleven
Goodnight-Loving   67

Twelve
Lincoln County War   74

Thirteen
The Shooter   81

Fourteen
The Kidnap   88

Fifteen
A Plea   91

Sixteen
The Cowboys' Last Ride   96

Seventeen
Last Night Home   103

Eighteen
Ride to Colorado   107

Nineteen
Alamosa Departure   114

Twenty
The Rock   117

Twenty-One
Durango   123

Twenty-Two
Rainstorm   130

Twenty-Three
Animas Crossing 133

Twenty-Four
The Riverbank 142

Twenty-Five
Homecoming 146

Twenty-Six
Return of an American Cowboy 149

Twenty-Seven
Epilogue 153

Preface

Who were the real cowboys who roamed the Southwest and protected the people? Movies have given us a vision of who they were in the forms of John Wayne and Clint Eastwood—tall, stoic men who beat all the odds to accomplish their goals.

This thought came to me when preparing to write a book about the West: Were the cowboys of the Old West really in the vision of Hollywood, or were they something else?

It turned out that Hollywood was right, but also wrong.

The cowboys of the Old West weren't the biggest guys around. They were average-sized men, one-third being of mixed race. These cowboys were hard-working, with few Wild West gun fights. However, they were men of character, ethics, and grit who stood tall when needed.

My search for a genuine cowboy led me directly to this story. A story of adventure, friendship, love, and sacrifice. This story led me to John, Frank, and Jane.

Their story became that of America post-Civil War, which was divided and wounded. People came to the Southwest after the war seeking a new start, a reclamation of their dreams for a better life, a new life altogether. A life far removed from the trauma of war and hatred. The Southwest allowed these people from all walks of life a genuine chance at that new life.

John, Frank, and Jane became part of the story about starting a new life out of the ashes of an old one. They became my vision for cowboys of the Southwest. The true cowboys who roamed the plains and risked everything they had to help others.

They defined what America was, and what she would become. The cowboys played a crucial role in building the foundation of this incredible country through their hard work, dedication, and unity.

This is my story of the American Cowboys.

ACR

One

El Paso Rescue

1890

Death faces every man. What makes a man is how he faces death.

This had always been Frank Morgan's motto in life. It drove him to persevere while living as a slave, escaping to freedom, and fighting for the North during the Civil War.

But now it was his child, his only child, who was facing death. There was a knife being held to his throat.

Holding the knife was Dane Manson, the evilest person in the West, the darkness of his eyes matched only by the darkness of his soul. Dane and Michael were in the main car of the hijacked El Paso train, while Frank was stuck in the adjoining car because of a jammed door and could only helplessly watch through the small window of the train car.

During the Battle of Tupelo, Frank had crossed paths with Dane, giving him a visible scar on his face. Dane, six feet tall, was a cold-blooded killer who fought for the South. But he was no match for Frank, who stood brooding at six feet three inches.

Inside the train car with Dane and Michael was Boyd Douglas, another American Cowboy. He had gotten the drop on Dane, but not before he had grabbed Michael. Boyd was also a Confederate veteran from the Civil War, but he despised Dane's ruthlessness. Boyd, five feet ten inches, was an average-sized cowboy with dark brown hair and brown eyes. He wanted to bring Dane to justice, but he did not want to jeopardize Michael's life by acting hastily. His range was too close for his Winchester rifle to make a safe shot. But Frank, not understanding Boyd's hesitancy, wanted him to act.

Michael was Frank's only child with his wife, Maybelle. In 1872, when Michael was only four, yellow fever had claimed her. He had promised her that he'd always take care of Michael. In 1878, Frank and his partner, John Rose, after they left the Lincoln County Regulators, founded the American Cowboys with one aim: to protect those who couldn't protect themselves. Their duties included, among others, rescuing hijacked trains. Michael had wanted to join the group and had begged his father, who reluctantly agreed. So, Michael became the youngest American Cowboys member at twenty-two years old.

With the rescue of the hijacked El Paso train going sour, he wished he had refused Michael that day.

"Drop your rifle or I'll cut the boy!" Dane yelled at Boyd.

The Cowboys had killed the other hijackers; Dane was the last one standing and the one they wanted the most. He was the leader of these train bandits who needed to be stopped. Frank, stuck in the adjoining car, could only watch. After dealing with the other hijackers, John and the other Cowboys—Oscar Martinez and Ben Weathers—were making their way to the main train car, unaware of what was unfolding inside.

Dane dug his knife into Michael's neck, causing him to moan in pain. Boyd finally relented—since he did not have a clear shot—and dropped his Winchester rifle.

Frank knew this was a deadly mistake by Boyd and that his son would pay the price. He could only watch helplessly as Dane cut Michael's throat from ear to ear, and as Michael fell to the floor the only noise louder than the steam engine's roar was Frank's scream.

Dane looked toward Frank and gave him his trademark wink.

Boyd picked up his rifle so he could shoot Dane—but it was too late: Dane had made his getaway to the back door of the train car and jumped off the train.

With all the strength he could muster, Frank smashed through the jammed door and ran to his son. He held his son's body as tight as he could and screamed, "Why?"

Boyd approached Frank to console him, but Frank quickly stood up and punched him in the face. Standing over Boyd he said, "If I ever see you again, I will take you out of this world." He paused. "You allowed that animal to kill my son."

The rest of the Cowboys, when they finally made it to the train car, were aghast. John and Ben tried to console Frank. "Neither of you know my pain. Save your words for someone else," he said in rebuke to his friends' attempts to console him. Oscar, Michael's best friend, went to his friend's dead body, fell to his knees, and began to cry.

The train car went on in eerie quietness until Frank said, "Michael isn't the only one who died today. The American Cowboys will ride no more."

He picked up Michael's body and went to a booth to mourn his dead child in private.

John knew things would never be the same for the American Cowboys.

Two

The Rose Ranch

The two-week journey from Texas to his home in Chama, located in the New Mexico Territory, seemed longer. John could not wait to embrace his beautiful wife, Jane. As he passed through the gate of their ranch, he saw her waiting in the distance, her long, blonde hair blowing in the cool wind.

Their ranch was ten acres with a sprawling landscape, situated in a small valley and surrounded by tall trees. John admired their property line, which seemed protected by the beautiful trees whose leaves were starting to change with the seasons. He had been fortunate to have a chance to purchase this property for himself and Jane, thanks to his life savings obtained from working security for railroad companies. The landscape surrounding their ranch house, which he had built himself, was rich with soil and helped them to grow crops to provide for themselves. The ranch had been his lifetime goal and had become a reality, and having Jane as his wife made it a dream come true.

Jane had been eagerly awaiting his return. She was greatly relieved to know that her cowboy was safely returning home.

Jane was close with the Morgans, and John knew that the news would be hard on his wife. He dismounted his horse and went to Jane, and she quickly wrapped her arms around him and kissed him. Every time he embraced Jane after returning from a trip, it felt like that first time on the dance floor at the Red River Railway train station in 1873. Their love had only grown stronger since then.

"I missed you so much, sweetie," John said.

"Were you gone? I hadn't noticed," Jane replied.

They laughed briefly before they kissed and embraced again. Then John knelt and kissed Jane's growing stomach. A few months before he'd left for the El Paso rescue, Jane had become pregnant. They had been trying for a while to have a baby.

"This is your father, little man. I'm ready to have you out here." They laughed again.

"I keep telling you," Jane said, "our princess will be out when she's ready."

He embraced Jane. They couldn't contain their happiness. But then he thought of Frank.

"Jane, I have some bad news. They killed Michael in El Paso."

"Oh my goodness! Please tell me it's not true."

"I wish it wasn't, Frank is devastated."

Shocked, Jane cried and held onto him even more tightly. She had been Michael's nanny when he was a boy. John knew that Frank must be feeling a much deeper sense of grief.

"Who killed him?" she asked.

"It was a man named Dane Manson; he rides for the Baron. They are both bad people."

While their lives were coming together, Frank's was falling apart. He had always been the father John wanted to be. Now that he was going to be a father, he could only hope to be half the father Frank had been to Michael. He had bravely raised his son on his own ever since he was widowed, refusing to remarry. He always said that he had vowed before God when he married Maybelle that he would never love another.

John respected everything Frank stood for and had accomplished. Since he was his role model, John knew he had big shoes to fill as a father. He had no other positive parental role model to look up to. His father, Charlie Rose, had been a belligerent drunk. When John was five, he'd seen his father beat his mother to death. When he received the news of his father's death in 1863 during the Civil War, John was relieved. How he died, John didn't know, but he was happy that his father was dead—he could never forgive him for what he had done to him and his mother, and he had almost let his rage consume him until, toward the end of the Civil War, a steady voice with a focus on faith in God had crossed his path. That voice belonged to Frank.

He offered John a message, one of determining your path and not allowing others to define your future. He quoted Romans 5:19, which discusses how one man's disobedience made many sinners and how one man's obedience can make many righteous. This helped John to grow closer to God, allowing him to let go of the hatred he had for his father. Frank gave him a green Bible, from which John learned the scripture, and he told him always to keep it close and turn to it often. He told John that a close friend gave him the Bible, and now he needed it. "One day," he told John, "you will give it to another needing to read God's word." John listened to his new friend and kept the Bible in his coat pocket. Eventually, his relationship with God transformed him into a new man, and he was grateful to Frank for sharing his faith with him.

And now John realized that he had to return the favor, and he vowed to do so. Frank had taught him and the rest of the Cowboys the most important promise they must make to each other—to never leave a fellow Cowboy behind.

As he started planning to go to Frank's home in Brazos, also in the New Mexico Territory, he remembered when he had met him for the first time—during the bloody days of the Civil War.

Their paths had crossed in Lee County, Mississippi, in 1864, and it would later come to be known as the Battle of Tupelo. Those bloody days had prepared them for their lives after the war.

Three

Battle of Tupelo

1864

July 14, 1864, was turning out to be a miserable day.

There was a smell of death in the air. Many men had already been killed in the fighting. The soldiers' eyes were burning from all the smoke created by cannon fire and the fields burning nearby. They had been set ablaze by the fighting that day. A soldier had to be careful about looking over the barriers for fear of being shot in the head. Death was not only in the air, it followed you in your thoughts and dreams.

The Confederate forces, led by Major General Nathan Bedford Forrest, had pinned John's regiment down. If General Forrest defeated the Union army, the Confederacy could access the Union supply lines in Tennessee, which would impede or halt Union Major General William T. Sherman's march on Atlanta.

To make matters worse, it was a brutally humid day in Mississippi. The temperature was, some of the Union scouts had informed John, over 100 degrees. The heat beat down on the Union soldiers, and victory seemed distant—it was going to be a humiliating loss, as they outnumbered the Confederacy in men by 14,000 to 8,000.

John was behind the Union barrier with his friend, Lieutenant Brody Sammons. Brody was two years older than John, and his heroic actions in previous battles had earned him his current position within the Union Army. He was about the same size as John, and he had long brown hair that flowed out of his army hat. The other officers gave Brody a hard time about his hair, but they came to accept it on account of the valor he fought with during battle.

"John," Brodie said, "we seem to be in a tough spot. I'm thinking about charging the rebels on the right. What do you think?"

John thought for a moment. "I think we better wait for General Smith to give us an advancement order. We don't want to compromise the regiment."

Brody had expected this response from his trusted friend. The proposition he'd made was born out of frustration. All the soldiers were frustrated and ready to fight. But unknown to their regiment, Union Major General Andrew J. Smith was leading Forrest toward this aggressive approach so they could flank his regiment. When John and Brody noticed the Union soldiers attacking the Confederate flank, they cheered. Soon after, the Union command gave the signal for the advance to begin.

"Let's get in the fight, men!" Brody said.

They started firing at the Confederate soldiers, and with every passing minute, it appeared that the Union might just turn the tide of this battle.

They fought valiantly. John and Brody's regiment quickly made it closer to the flanking Union regiment. Once they were face to face, they were stunned to see that their Union counterparts were, in fact, United States Colored Troops. Up to this point in the war, they had only heard about having colored troop regiments, never actually seeing the regiment themselves. This did not stop their momentum as they continued their advance toward the Confederate front.

John was impressed by the focused determination of the Colored Troops. They were fighting as if they were fighting for their freedom, which they were. This inspired John to fight even harder so they could defeat General Forrest.

One man, John noticed, seemed like a man among boys: a black sergeant from the Colored Troops, engaged in hand-to-hand combat with the Confederate troops. He could see the fear in their eyes as this man easily beat them one by one.

Then, a Confederate squared up to the sergeant while he was in the middle of a fight and took a swing at him with a sword. The sergeant dodged the attack and struck the Confederate on the left cheek with a small knife.

"Dane is in trouble!" another Confederate yelled. "Someone needs to kill that Yankee."

From his gray and red jacket, John knew this was the infamous Dane, who had been mutilating the surrendering Union soldiers. According to legend, he wore the bicolored jacket to symbolize the Confederacy or death. The sergeant punched Dane in the face as hard as he could before dropping for cover, as two Confederate soldiers began firing at him.

While the sergeant waited for the gunfire to subside, Dane retreated to the Confederate lines. John felt that this would not be the last time he would see the infamous Dane. Evil, he thought, is hard to kill, and Dane had the reputation of being the Devil himself.

The sergeant's ability and passion on the battlefield had inspired John. He fought harder than before from his example and, before long, they were side by side, fighting the Confederate soldiers and driving them back.

Then, feeling as if someone had punched him in his right arm, John fell to the ground. He didn't know who had hit him; his immediate line was all Union soldiers. He reached his left hand up to his throbbing right arm and discovered that, after being in the army for months, someone had finally managed to shoot him. Since there was not sufficient medical care offered to the wounded, soldiers feared being shot. He tried to remember his training and what he'd been taught about caring for such wounds. Then it hit him that he might lose his arm. If their arms or legs got injured, some of the soldiers had to have amputations.

"If you're not dead, then get up and fight!" a deep voice said.

John looked up. It was the man who had been fighting so valiantly. Now that they were looking at each other, John could see the determination in his eyes. On that battlefield, he was a big man, and he had eyes of steel. He stuck his hand out to John to help him get up.

"Death faces every man," he said. "What makes a man is how he faces death. Will you face death sitting in this field, or will you do it fighting for our great nation?"

He grabbed the man's hand and pulled himself up.

"I'm Frank Morgan, and today we make history."

"I'm John Rose, nice to meet you."

They resumed fighting the Confederates, with John's pain quickly becoming an afterthought. They fought side by side on that bloody battlefield. Finally, once the Confederates were in full retreat, cheers rang out. Everyone in the two regiments knew who the hero of the day was: Frank. He earned everyone's respect on the battlefield that day.

***

While John was getting his wound treated in the medical tent, Frank entered and sat next to him.

"Great fighting today," Frank said.

"Thank you, but you led us to victory today," John replied.

"Trust me, no one won today. Many people lost family on that battlefield."

Both men sat silently for a moment. The scars they had endured, both physically and mentally, would be their burden to carry. These men weren't just fighting a war, they were fighting countrymen.

"How are you holding up, other than your arm?" Frank asked.

"About as good as the rest of the men."

"Do you have a family?" Frank asked.

"None living, just myself and my regiment."

"I am the same way; except I have the Lord with me."

"The Lord? Are you a preacher?" John replied.

"We are all preachers, brother." This inspired a laugh from John. Frank reached into his coat and pulled out a green Bible. "Our God gives us great wisdom and strength, found in this book."

This comment confused him. "I am surprised to hear you talk about God, being such a ferocious soldier," John replied.

"The two go hand in hand. Have you ever read God's word?" Frank asked.

John did not know how to answer this question. He always blamed God for his mother being killed by his father. He did not understand how a god could let her suffer that fate. "Honestly, I have never wanted to read it."

Frank paused before saying, "I understand. Do you think God doesn't care about you?"

"I know he doesn't. My mother died at the hands of a violent man. How could a god care about us and let that happen?" He didn't like this discussion about God. He would have walked out of the tent if the doctors had finished tending his wound. At the moment, however, they were busy working on other soldiers who required more attention.

Frank gave it a moment. He could sense John was upset by his cold behavior. "Do you know how many friends and family I saw getting killed in front of me in Mississippi?"

This caught John off guard. He slowly looked at him and shook his head from side to side, signaling that he did not.

"I witnessed three people being beaten to death right in front of me by the same evil man."

Sitting motionless on the gurney, John could only look at Frank. He was speechless.

"The plantation owners wanted us to watch, so we would learn to follow the rules. Do you know what I learned from those experiences?"

"No, please tell me."

"I learned God is good."

Puzzled, John replied, "God is good, with people being beaten to death in front of you?"

Frank leaned into him and replied, "Because they set my people free when they died. The next second, they were with God."

"How do you know?"

"Because God's word says it is so. You just have to read it."

Still doubting his new friend, he said, "What does it say about death?"

"Let me tell you," Frank said while opening his Bible and turning the pages until he stopped when he found the passage.

He then read Psalm 23, which says, *"Even though I walk through the valley of the shadow of death, I will fear no evil, for you are with me; your rod and your staff, they comfort me. You prepare a table before me in the presence of my enemies; you anoint my head with oil; my cup overflows. Surely goodness and mercy shall follow me all the days of my life, and I shall dwell in the house of the Lord forever."*

The men sat quietly, thinking about the words Frank had read. John, for the first time in his life, wanted to know more about what else God had to say.

"Can you read some more?" he said finally.

Laughing, Frank replied, "I will do you one better. Take this Bible and read it. Every man needs a Bible close to him."

John took the green Bible into his hands. It was a little worn from being used but felt smooth in his hands. Looking at Frank, he said, "I can't take your Bible; that wouldn't be right."

"I have another; besides, a good man gave me that Bible years ago on the condition I give it to another who needs it at the correct time. I ask you to do the same."

Looking down at the Bible, John became emotional at the gesture from his new friend. "Thank you. How will I know when to give it away?"

"You will know. Just like I did today."

The men looked at one another and smiled. Both realized they had made a godly connection. From the horror and bloodshed of war emerged a peaceful and strong bond.

When Brody entered the tent and shouted John's name, he put an end to the peaceful spirit.

"I'm in the back corner, Brody," John said.

Brody, upon seeing him, quickly made his way to the gurney. "We need to go right now. There's a train we must stop. It's heading to Brice's Corner Road, ten miles to the north of us."

"What's on this train, Lieutenant?" Frank asked.

"It's not what's on it. If they find out we've taken Tupelo, they'll get word to Confederate reinforcements, and the rebels could overwhelm us. This entire war could be lost."

Frank looked at John and nodded, then looked to Brody and said, "How many men do we need?"

"We need five men. John will be the fourth man. All we need is one more."

"Look no further, I'm your fifth man," Frank said.

"Thank you, after today we will be glad to have you," Brody said.

The men left the medical tent after Brody ordered a doctor to finish John's arm, then they prepared their horses and quickly rode to Brice's Corner Road.

***

Just one month earlier, in June, the Confederates had earned a decisive victory at Brice's Corner Road. This gave them control of the railway running by the road. It also led to the Battle of Tupelo.

Once the men were in position with their horses, they hid among the trees and waited.

"Have you men ever boarded a train?" Brody asked. Frank and John shook their heads no. The other two men were Will and James. James was as quiet as a mouse but as mean as a bobcat by reputation. He was ready for this challenge but also did not have experience boarding a train.

"Will, how about you?" Brody asked.

"Yes, sir, I have boarded a train. It's not enjoyable, but I'm here." He'd fought against the rebels in the June battle. Will would just as soon have gone home; he was tired of this war.

"Great, I am the lead man. Will, you board second, so we can get two men on the train quickly. John will board third then James fourth. Frank, I want you to go last. I need someone with the strength of a bear covering our rear."

"Yes sir, Lieutenant."

Brody nodded and then explained how to complete the challenging task. He explained they would ride out of the trees and stay close to the train. It was dark and the night would help to give them cover from being seen. They were not expecting Confederate scouts on the train, since they did not know they had lost Tupelo.

Then, one at a time, they would ride up to the side ladder on the caboose, jump from the horse to the ladder, and then immediately cover the caboose doors. The Confederate soldiers would be in the caboose on this five-car train they were boarding. The five cars comprised the engine, coal car, two equipment cars, and, finally, the caboose. They would subdue the soldiers, and then take the engine by overwhelming the train engineers.

"One warning—get close enough to the ladder to jump onto it, but not too close or the horse may get knocked into the wheels," Brody said. The men all nodded in agreement.

In the distance, the men heard the undeniable sound of a train engine approaching. John was nervous. This would be a first for him. He tightened his grip on the reins and prepared himself for what he assumed would be chaos. Brody gave the signal, and all of their horses were soon galloping toward the train tracks. The soldiers were quickly next to the train as Brody made his move to board the train. Brody's ease and skill in lunging from his horse, grabbing the side ladder rails, and quickly positioning himself near the caboose doors impressed John.

Next was Will. He was not as lucky. John noticed he was further away from the side ladder than Brody had been. He couldn't jump properly because his boot got caught in the stirrup. Even though brief, it was enough to cause him to miss the ladder and disappear under the train wheels. He was gone. Shocked, John tensed up, hoping to not have the same outcome.

Now it was his turn. John's heart was racing faster than the horse's hooves pattering on the ground. He closed in near the side ladder. This was the moment of truth. With his injured arm, this would be difficult. Just as John was preparing to jump, he felt a lump in his side pocket. It was the green Bible. He thought about Frank, the scripture from Psalms, and about dying. Then John did something new to him. He prayed, asking God to deliver him safely through this mission, strengthen his arm to hold his weight and give him courage. John knew the time was now, being next to the ladder, but not too close. He lunged for it and made it. Once aboard, he got into position. Brody was slightly ahead of him and nodded his approval. He thanked God for delivering him safely onto the train. James, then Frank, easily boarded the train. The men were ready. With one man short, they would have to be perfect to take the train. John thought that if God had gotten them on the train, then the rest would be easy.

The men busted into the caboose, and a shootout ensued. It was quickly over as they had systematically taken out the soldiers. Sadly, James met his end as he was shot and killed. They would only have three men to take the engine. The men strategically made their way to the engine. To their surprise, the Confederates only had one engineer aboard. Brody easily subdued him, and the train was theirs. They slowed the train to a halt. After a few minutes, a group of Union train engineers approached the motionless train. They had been waiting in the hope that the men could successfully take the train. Seeing they had been successful, the engineers proceeded to the train and spoke with Brody. Then, they boarded the train for inspection.

The three men were excited yet relieved after finishing the daring mission. After gathering their horses, they were soon back at camp in Tupelo. Brody excused himself so he could go to headquarters and report what had happened. Before leaving, he went to Frank.

"You are one heck of a soldier; you can ride with me anytime."

"I would be much obliged Lieutenant, just say the word." They shook hands, then Brody left the camp. John and Frank sat at a campfire to contemplate the unbelievable day they had endured. The battle and the train mission alone were experiences for a lifetime, much less one day. They finally had some time to talk and get to know more about each other.

Frank's passion for life, John discovered, was contagious. They discussed plans for what they could do after the war. They both agreed on the importance of protecting those who could not protect themselves. They wanted to assemble a group of men who could protect people and systems from nefarious individuals. One such system was the railway. The Civil War had more than adequately revealed the importance of the railroad to the war effort.

Then they started discussing why they had joined the war.

"I wanted to guarantee America's long-lasting future," John said. "I even joined the war early, when I was sixteen." What had happened to his mother drove John to protect people. He felt that was what he was doing in the war.

Frank's story was quite different and made John respect him even more.

Four

Frank

1861

Frank clearly remembered the beatings received from the plantation owners.

The last one was because he stopped working in the fields to care for his friend Jimmy, who had collapsed while working. Jimmy had not been feeling well and was suffering from headaches. The headaches, he told Frank, were so bad it felt like his head was a melon being split open. When they became severe, he would faint. Jimmy, who had been raised on the plantation, was twenty; he was six feet tall and had a muscular build. Jimmy and Frank were two of the strongest slaves, and the plantation owners worked them hard. He always remembered that day—it was the first time they whipped Jimmy.

Two years later, Jimmy was being tied up for another beating— he had passed out in the fields again. Because of his worsening headaches, the plantation owners shifted him from the group of hard laborers to that of the cotton gatherers. But being out in the heat did not help his headaches at all, and his health rapidly declined.

Big Tommy had become the man to deliver beatings on the plantation. He was big, strong, and unforgiving with his punishment. The plantation owners wanted someone to punish the slaves so severely that the others would learn to comply with their rules. Big Tommy had shown them he was the man for the job through the savage beatings he delivered. As he was getting ready to whip Jimmy, he said, "Jimmy, I am going to beat those headaches out of you one way or the other." Most of the slaves on the plantation were present for this beating because the plantation owners insisted that they watch the beatings. The plantation owners felt it would be a lesson for everyone who considered escaping work. The owners didn't care if the slaves had health issues—they only cared that the work was done.

Frank was near Jimmy and could feel the anger building within himself at the thought of his friend being beaten again. Once Big Tommy started beating Jimmy, Frank tightened his hands into fists. He was so tired of the beatings—they had to stop. With every lash on Jimmy's back, Frank squeezed his fists harder. By the sixth lash, he noticed that Jimmy appeared to pass out. Then Frank saw it: blood oozing from Jimmy's mouth, his eyes wide open. Tears streamed down Frank's cheeks. He feared the worst.

Finally, the lashes only stopped at the insistence of the plantation owner because Jimmy was not moving. Just as he feared, Jimmy was dead.

Big Tommy laughed. "Well, I fixed his headaches."

The plantation owners laughed, and Frank's anger grew with each laugh. His days of living on the plantation, he decided, had to end.

Frank couldn't take being enslaved anymore. He and eight others had been planning an escape for weeks, and Jimmy's death sparked their resolve to flee from this hell. They planned to escape on a

Sunday night because the plantation owners took the day to rest and most of the guards were not present until Monday morning.

The plantation was in Senatobia, Mississippi, and was massive at 1,900 acres. It was hot and muggy in Mississippi during the summer. There were rolling hills throughout the area, which had some areas of dense tree coverage. Making your way around the area at nighttime could be difficult if you are not familiar with the terrain. Fortunately for Frank, he had lived in this area long enough to know the terrain and could easily navigate at nighttime—as could most of the other slaves. The air was thick at nighttime from the humidity and still uncomfortable due to the heat. The escape would be challenging—but worth the risk.

On Sunday night, the group quietly snuck out of the living quarters and stepped toward freedom. Everything went according to plan, and soon they only had to clear one more area of the plantation; after that, freedom was theirs. But this was the hardest part because Big Tommy guarded the outer gates. When the group neared the gates, they crouched down, and as they inched closer, they could make out the shape of a large man standing near the fence line of the plantation's outer perimeter.

Big Tommy was six foot three and easily weighed over two hundred and fifty pounds. Frank, despite being of the same height, was not as big as Big Tommy, who was older and more filled out. If Big Tommy discovered them, Frank knew he was the one who must confront him. He valued his group's freedom more than his own, and he was ready to sacrifice himself for them. They would have to be quiet to avoid alerting Big Tommy that they were attempting to escape the plantation. Big Tommy's job while guarding the plantation fence line at night was to notify other plantation workers that slaves were escaping by ringing the large bell that was positioned near the fence line by the gates to the plantation. The bell was large —three feet tall—and when ringing could be heard throughout the plantation. The bell had previously been positioned at the top of an old missionary bell tower and had been removed by the plantation owner so it could be positioned at the front gate for the guard to ring if there were problems. If Big Tommy rang the bell, armed men would swarm to the gates in minutes. He vowed to not let Big Tommy ring that bell no matter what.

One by one, the group slipped past Big Tommy and went through the gate. The plan after passing this area was to meet one mile north of the plantation. There, they would gather the supplies left by supporters of the underground railroad and make a desperate run for free lands by following the Mississippi River. To ensure that everyone made it out safely, Frank agreed to go last. Soon, in front of him, there were only two others. Freedom was almost theirs.

Suddenly, about twenty yards ahead of Frank, there was a roar.

Joe Mince had caused it—he had accidentally tripped on a bundle of logs.

"Who goes there?" shouted Big Tommy.

All was quiet for a moment until Big Tommy moved toward the logs.

Joe was sixty-two and weighed about one hundred and forty pounds. He was, Frank knew, no match for Big Tommy.

Big Tommy moved closer to Joe. The entire group was now moments away from being caught.

Frank knew he had to intervene now.

One positive for Frank about his circumstances was that he had grown up hearing God's word. His people were people of faith. Through their witness, he had become a follower of Christ. He valued his relationship with God. Some days, God's word was the only thing that kept him going. He needed God's intervention now more than ever. He turned to the scripture for courage.

Psalms 41:10: *Fear not, for I am with you; be not dismayed, for I am your God; I will strengthen you, I will help you, I will uphold you with my righteous right hand.*

Frank was fighting for freedom, and God, he believed, was on his side.

As he lay on the ground, waiting to be found by Big Tommy, Joe knew that death was close. Though he was prepared to fight, he knew he was no match for Big Tommy.

But just before Big Tommy discovered Joe, there was a noise: it resembled a wild boar rushing through the brush.

It was Frank charging at Big Tommy.

Big Tommy never knew what hit him. He was down on the ground and stunned as Frank got on top of him and beat him. As he punched him over and over, Frank remembered Big Tommy beating Jimmy. He'd witnessed at least three people die from his beatings, including Jimmy. On this night, Frank was finally getting vengeance for the beatings he had witnessed Big Tommy perform on his people.

To Frank's surprise, with his right hand, Big Tommy punched him on the left side of his face. He threw Frank off him and ran to the gate bell. Everyone's freedom, Frank knew, came down to this moment. He had to choose between killing or being killed. He grabbed a medium-sized log and went after Big Tommy. With about ten yards to go until Big Tommy reached the bell, Frank caught him and smashed the log over his head, and Big Tommy fell to the ground. Then Frank put him in a headlock and choked him. Big Tommy put up a great struggle at first, but then slowly weakened until he was motionless. Frank didn't release his hold until he was certain that Big Tommy was dead. And when he was, Frank released the arm around his neck and fell onto his back. He was overwhelmed with emotion. Big Tommy was the face of tyranny to the slaves, and now that he was dead, Frank felt the emotional weight of the struggle his people had been through rush out of him, and he cried.

He felt a hand on his shoulder, and he looked up.

"It's time to go, brother," Joe said. "You did your people proud, but the journey is far from over."

Frank nodded his head in agreement. Joe helped him to his feet, and they started their journey north to meet the others. He asked God to forgive him for what he had done to Big Tommy, but he thanked Him for helping them escape the plantation and head for freedom.

That freedom would be realized when they could see the Clock Tower Church in New Albany, Indiana.

Five

The Clock Tower Church

The journey to freedom is a hard road for escaping slaves.

With the summer ending, only one of the original eight slaves escaping with Frank to the free territories in the North remained. Four had turned back to the plantation after a few days of travel. The brutally hot weather and the stress of being sought were too difficult for them. They faced severe punishment from the plantation owners, especially with Frank killing Big Tommy. Three others had died along the way. One had drowned in the Mississippi when their first boat turned over. They had taken refuge in Tennessee for a few days following the boat incident. Then one evening, a farm owner stumbled upon the group while they were sleeping in the brush. He shot two of them as they attempted to flee. They stayed on the Mississippi River after that.

Their journey would end in the free state of Indiana. There were few travel options for escaping slaves, thanks in part to the distance they had to travel and the many slave states they would have to pass through. They traveled up the Mississippi River posing as laborers on a boat. The Mississippi eventually merged into the Ohio River, which would take them to their destination, New Albany, Indiana.

New Albany was home to the Town Clock Church and had become a beacon of hope to slaves seeking freedom. The clock tower on the church rose to a staggering 160 feet, making it easily visible to approaching visitors. Once the fleeing slaves saw this towering church steeple, they knew freedom was theirs. The joy of freedom would not come, however, until setting foot on the Indiana side of the Ohio River, because on the other side of the river was the slave state of Kentucky. Frank pondered the fleeting nature of freedom when it was merely separated by a river.

Joe was the other slave to make it this far with Frank. Now, he was sick with pneumonia and dying. Frank did what he could to make Joe comfortable. The goal was to get him to Indiana. They were close, but it was difficult to tell where they were because of the darkness on the Ohio River, due to the cloudy night.

"Joe, hang in there, brother. We are almost to New Albany."

Coughing, Joe weakly responded, "I am trying to hold on. It is getting harder to breathe."

Frank knew Joe would not last much longer. He just prayed that Joe could make it to the shores of Indiana and plant his feet on free soil. Then, as if caused by a breath of air from the Almighty, the clouds cleared. The moonlight was bright, lighting up the river and the shores. Frank was worried momentarily that residents of Kentucky may see the boat and come after them. He was nervous about being seen by Southerners this close to freedom. Suddenly, thanks to the light of the moon, he could see the steeple. Fears of Southerners quickly disappeared from his mind as the tall clock tower captured Frank's attention.

With tears filling his eyes, he said, "Joe, we're here brother, there is the clock tower."

Joe raised his head and said, "That is a beautiful sight. Get me inside the church as soon as we dock the boat."

Frank was full of emotions when the boat finally docked at the New Albany pier. The journey had been difficult, with many tough losses along the way. Finally being in a free state was a relief, but the path to reach there would haunt him for the rest of his days. He helped Joe get to his feet, then exited the boat and started walking toward the Clock Tower Church. The towering steeple grew taller as the men approached the church. Their contacts with the underground railroad had assured them they would be safe in the church. A sign was on the outside of the building announcing that an evening service would begin soon. Frank and Joe made it to the doors and entered. It had an attractive sanctuary that was painted white, and two dozen wooden pews lined the interior with a few people sitting upon them. There was a wooden pulpit in front of the church with a cross on its front. Frank helped Joe to a pew at the back of the church and sat down. Joe was having difficulty breathing and pulled Frank close to him.

"Thank you, Frank, we are free men."

"Yes, we are. It was a tiresome journey, but now we are free," he responded while putting his arm around Joe.

"Now let me rest. My journey has been long, and the reward is freedom," Joe said weakly before slumping over onto Frank. He knew Joe had just died. The man who had been by his side since leaving Mississippi was now gone. He was thankful to have gotten him to free land before he died.

A pastor entered from behind the pulpit of the church, carrying a green Bible, and made his way to the pulpit for the evening service. He was a man of small stature with a slight paunch. The pastor noticed Frank at the back of the church and Joe slumped over next to him. He smiled toward him and then opened his Bible.

The pastor welcomed everyone to the service and announced he would read from the book of Isaiah. Frank looked around the church, taking inventory of the occupants. All were black and had the same appearance he did, with tattered clothes. He assumed they had also recently arrived here after fleeing the South. As the preacher was beginning his sermon, he reflected on everything that had happened that led him to this church. There were so many deaths, doubts about being able to make it to Indiana, and now Joe was dead. He immediately became resolute that he would never return to the South again. Some people he'd met during his journey north mentioned that Canada was the best place to go. Canada sounded good.

The preacher caught Frank's attention when he heard him say, "Freedom is a gift that should be shared with others." This statement intrigued Frank and caused him to leave his thoughts about fleeing to Canada so he could focus on the preacher's words. The preacher then said, "If God brought you this far, then you have been blessed." He paused after looking at Frank, then continued by saying, "Now it is your godly duty to help share this liberty with others." The preacher referenced Isaiah 61:1, which says, *"The spirit of the Lord God is upon me, Because the Lord has anointed me to bring good news to the afflicted; He has sent me to bind up the brokenhearted, to proclaim liberty to captives and freedom to prisoners."* This passage left Frank stunned. He'd been so lost in the trials of the journey to freedom that he had lost sight of the fact of how many others were still in slavery in the South. Those people all deserved to have freedom, as he now did.

Three black women then came into the church from the door behind the pulpit, and the preacher motioned them over to him. He whispered something to them, and they looked in Frank's direction. This caused his entire body to become tense. After being on the run for so long, he questioned everyone's motives. The women made their way to Frank. He was ready for anything.

"I think we need to help you with your friend," one woman said to Frank. "I think he has passed."

He was relieved that they were trying to help. "Yes, ma'am, he had a mighty journey, but now he is home."

As they began taking care of Joe, Frank stood up to give them room. The preacher was finishing his message and thanked everyone for attending. He briefly mentioned that the church provided a warm meal and a place to rest in the home next door. Then he made his way over to the women tending to Joe.

He turned around and said to Frank, "Welcome to Clock Tower Church. I'm Pastor Clerkly. How are you doing, brother?"

"I'm doing as best as I can. Thank you for helping with Joe."

"You're welcome. Now I want you to take this." He handed Frank his green Bible. Frank looked at the Bible and then back at the pastor.

"Pastor, are you sure I can have this?"

"Yes, my brother, I have more, and you came here with nothing. Every man needs a Bible he can hold on to. Keep it close to you and turn to it often for guidance."

Nodding his head in agreement, Frank replied, "Thank you, brother Clerkly, I appreciate your kindness."

"I received this Bible some time ago. Now, I am passing it to you. One day you will give it to someone needing to read God's word."

Pastor Clerkly smiled at him, patted his shoulder, then turned and left through the same door he had entered. Frank smiled and looked toward the cross near the pulpit and was grateful for the message he had heard. He then exited the church with his prized possession. The only thing he now owned, as a freeman, was a Bible.

After leaving the church, Frank began walking toward the house to get something to eat. A warm meal would be good after the long ride on the boat. He was reflecting on the pastor's message and people still enslaved in the South. There had to be a way to help get them to freedom. The underground railroad was a worthy cause, it just could not help everyone.

"Our brothers and sisters need your help; the time is now to help bring them freedom," he heard a voice saying. The voice belonged to a tall black man speaking to a few people standing near the back of the church. Frank paused momentarily to listen to the man. "Who else do we trust to bring freedom to our people other than ourselves?" the man continued. "We have been given the gift of freedom, and now it's our responsibility to share it with others." Frank's emotions built up inside of him. These were powerful words and made him realize his journey did not end simply by making it to Indiana. He made his way over to the man who was speaking. Frank had to know what he could do to help ensure the slaves of the South achieved their liberty as he had. As if the man knew Frank's thoughts, he said, "The way we can help is by getting into the fight and joining the US Colored Troops. This is our chance to make a difference." The man was enlisting people to sign up with the colored regiments to help fight in the war. The US government had recently approved this for the coming year, 1862.

Frank had not considered this and had planned to keep moving north to Canada. Now he had a decision to make, go north and leave this strife behind, or join the fight to help others gain freedom. Then he remembered the pastor's message from Isaiah 61, mentioning how the Lord anoints to bring good news to the afflicted, to bind up the broken-hearted, and to proclaim liberty to captives and freedom to prisoners. He thought back to Jimmy and him being beaten to death, the people who had died on their journey to Indiana, and, finally, he remembered Joe. With tears streaming down his cheeks, Frank looked up and said, "God, anoint me to help my brothers and sisters imprisoned. Use me to proclaim liberty and help them have freedom." After a pause, he said, "Take my life and help me give others the gift of freedom."

Frank was emotional and took a moment to collect himself. He now had a mission in his life to strive for, not for himself but for others who could not fight for themselves.

Frank walked up to the man speaking to enlist with the US Colored Troops.

Six

The Baron

1890

The Baron sat in his dark office at his ranch in Alamosa, Colorado, growing madder with each strike of the clock. He had just received word that Navajo Chief Lonewolf had refused his offer to buy their land. The Baron rubbed his salt and pepper hair out of frustration. He was 55 years old and felt every bit of it. The extra weight he'd put on didn't help him feel any better. His love of food was catching up with him. He hailed from New York and was used to relishing hearty Italian cuisine. It was also in New York that he'd gained the knack for making money.

From early on, he'd discovered his ability to make a lot of money through corruption and intimidation, exploiting any chance to make quick profits, unconcerned with ethics or the impact of his actions on others. Soon, he became a successful businessman, one who operated in the shadows, and amassed a fortune. If the Baron knew there were opportunities to make money, he would take them.

Almost all the money he had made vanished in the panic of 1873. Until that happened, he had thought that his days spent struggling for wealth were behind him. The Long Depression, as it was called, was a financial crisis that affected Americans and Europeans. As the economy recessed, the Baron's net worth also eroded.

He hoped to rebuild his wealth through the railway business. He despised those who stood in the railway's way that he planned to build, just as he despised those who criticized him for being a carpetbagger after the Civil War.

To rebuild his wealth, he first used his connections in the financial world. He started as a tax collector in the Southern states, but the residents despised him. Soon, he realized he needed a better and faster way to rebuild his wealth, one that did not involve the headache of dealing with Southerners. The best way, he decided, was to become a railroad tycoon. He aimed to compete with the associates in the railway business—Leland Stanford, Collis Hunting-ton, Charles Crocker, and Mark Hopkins—and establish a railway like the Union Pacific Railroad, which was completed in 1869. He despised JP Morgan and wanted him out of the railway business. Morgan was one of the top financier bankers in the United States and used his power to undermine the leading railroad businessman, Jay Cooke. This drove Cooke and his business partners to their collective financial collapse. Afterward, JP Morgan took it upon himself to intervene in the railway business, to create a national railroad empire through reorganization and consolidation. Morgan was hoping to stop a rate war and limit railway competition, which would drive up costs for consumers and increase profits for him. JP Morgan's principal goal seemed to be to secure his position as the lone railroad tycoon and prevent others from competing with him. To the Baron, Morgan was just another barrier that stood in his way from regaining his wealth. Morgan had become his chief nemesis and his principal obstacle to becoming a railroad tycoon. The Baron thus did anything in his power to skirt government regulations, JP Morgan, and build his railroad. Now, the Navajo had complicated the situation.

A loud knock at the door snapped him out of his angry state. "Whoever it is, come in!" the Baron said, sternly.

Dane entered with a scowl on his face. He knew, after the disaster of the El Paso robbery, he was going to have a hard conversation with the Baron. They could not get the valuables they were looking for and had caused collateral damage by killing Michael Morgan. Dane knew that Michael's father, Frank, would be out for blood. Now the question in his mind was, would the Baron let him live for this failure, or was he about to die? They did not want any unnecessary attention to their upcoming plans in the New Mexico Territory, but this was exactly that.

"Well, I see you made a mess in Texas," the Baron said.

Dane paused for a moment to ensure he had the correct response. "We had no other choice than to take out Frank's kid."

"What you did was draw the attention of the American Cowboys. There will be hell to pay for your decision."

To avoid upsetting his boss, Dane paused before he spoke again. "I can handle Frank and the rest of the American Cowboys. You just take care of everything on your end, and we will be okay."

The Baron looked at Dane with frustration, but he also knew there wasn't anyone else he could trust with this endeavor—he needed someone with a special, coldhearted viciousness to pull off the plan he had devised. Dane had lived a hard life surrounded by misery and death, and that made him the man for the plan.

Dane killed just about anything that walked the Earth. As a toddler, after losing his parents, he had to live with an abusive aunt and uncle, who, under the influence of alcohol, frequently beat him. When he was eleven, his demented aunt repeatedly hit him in the head and almost killed him. Dane was never the same after that incident and was quick to anger. As a teenager, his uncle taught him the evilness of plantation life. His uncle also forced Dane to take part in beating slaves—even killing them. Whites, his uncle taught him, were superior to slaves and they should be treated accordingly. Dane grew up with that mentality and found plenty of opportunities to apply it when he fought for the Confederacy in the Civil War, not missing any chance to kill Union soldiers, especially the freed blacks. Union soldiers killing his uncle and burning down their plantation solidified his hatred for blacks. Then something changed when he confronted Frank at Tupelo; he grudgingly acknowledged to himself that Frank could have killed him that day. Since then, he had been driven more by retribution than hatred. That retribution was for Frank.

After the war, he met up with the Baron while he was carpet-bagging. The Baron was fearful of bitter Confederates who sought retribution for losing the Civil War by trying to kill him. So, the Baron felt safer with a group of killers around him, and Dane was the perfect killer, for he was the most cold-blooded of them all. Likewise, Dane felt that the only way he could truly continue his vicious lifestyle was to work for the Baron, who could offer him a sense of superiority with his money and manpower. This was the only relationship he had with him. He was free to do what he wanted, and the Baron would ensure that no one held him accountable.

Now what he wanted, more than anything, was to kill Frank Morgan. Killing his son was bittersweet. Knowing Frank was suffering made him happy. However, he wanted Frank dead. That was the retribution he sought.

"Chief Lonewolf refused the offer to sell their land. We will have to make adjustments to the plan," the Baron said.

"Just take their land. They cannot stop us," Dane replied.

"We cannot just take the land, it must be given or sold to us, so we have the land rights. JP Morgan would find great pleasure in coming and taking this land for himself." The Baron felt he had JP Morgan beat at getting the Navajo land if the US Cavalry became involved. When this happened, the Cavalry gave the determination of who got the land rights to the territorial governing board. The governing board was in Alamosa, Colorado, and the Baron had hand-picked each one for those positions. They would reward him with the land, and JP Morgan could do nothing about it.

"How about you let me round up some boys and go force that Indian chief to sign an agreement? We can take a few of his fingers if he refuses." Dane was oblivious to his boss's master plan. The Baron, not fully trusting Dane with that information, played off Dane's ill-advised idea to attack the Navajo.

"Do you realize the Navajos outnumber our men ten to one? They would kill every one of you. I need the land, but we do not have the numbers to take it by force. The US Cavalry had a difficult time attempting that feat."

"What will we do then, boss?"

The Baron had a unique plan of his own. For too long, he'd had to wait to build the railway that he was sure would catapult him among the elite. His frustration grew when he faced resistance. He could not take the route of just building the railway like the associates—he wanted to be daring.

His plan hinged on causing, or manufacturing, an Indian uprising, then involving the US Cavalry. The Baron would instruct Dane to prepare for the main part of the plan: the kidnapping of Nizhoni, the daughter of the Navajo chief, Lonewolf. This, he thought, would bring the Navajos around to accepting a new deal. Two choices would be given to them. Sign the proposal, giving the land to the Baron, or Nazhoni would be killed. The Baron believed the Navajo would give in and sign the proposal. However, they would get no money from the Baron. It was personal now since they had refused his first offer. This had always been his practice as a ruthless businessman. Also, he needed to strike fear into other tribes in the area that may want to cause his railway any problems. He would have the Navajo come to his northern ranch in Silverton, Colorado. With the bluffs surrounding the town, his men would ambush the Navajo from the higher ground. It would be like shooting chickens in a cage. Then, they could frame the entire situation as a massive Navajo attack. That would force the US Cavalry to take action and eliminate the threat. Then the government would allow more advancement of the railways for progressive expansion into the West. The inevitable ruling from the New Mexico territorial governing board would give the rights to the Baron. His business tactics of violence and corruption would pave the way for him to reclaim his wealth.

There was a knock at the door. It was Barbara, the Baron's assistant. She apologized for the interruption. She had a message for Dane: the ranch hands needed him in the bunkhouse.

After Dane left for the bunkhouse, the Baron thought about the mass expansion of his railway, which would be possible if they pulled off his plan. The opportunities he would finally have would allow him to establish himself as a railroad tycoon. He became giddy when he thought of the riches that would come his way and the respect he would gain from the associates.

He went to his desk and stared at the map of the area where his new railway would be—from Texas through the New Mexico Territory and up into Colorado.

Imagining his evil scheme coming to fruition, he smiled from ear to ear.

Seven

Navajo

Chief Lonewolf had to persuade the Navajo tribe of the risks of accepting the Baron's proposal to use Navajo land for a new railway. The Baron offered the Navajo tribe a significant amount of money to give up their land. This was an insult to Chief Lonewolf, as he knew this land was not theirs to give away. The land belonged to the Navajo people who had come before them and those who would come after they were gone. So they refused the Baron's offer but did it respectfully—he was not one to take rejection well. The tribe couldn't afford a repeat of the Navajo wars. Chief Lonewolf wanted to protect the tribe's proud heritage and peacefully preserve their lands.

The Navajo had lived in modern-day Canada for many years. Once their people could travel south, they migrated to what would become the northwestern New Mexico Territory and areas of Colorado. They were hunters and gatherers by tradition. In Colorado, the Pueblo people taught them how to use crop-farming techniques. The Pueblo also taught them how to grow traditional foods such as corn, beans, and squash. When the Spanish explorers arrived, the

Navajos began keeping and herding livestock, such as sheep and goats, which became one of their primary sources of trade and food. They usually maintained peace with their neighboring tribes, but everything changed after the Navajo wars.

In 1849, US Military Governor Colonel John Washington negotiated a treaty with Navajo forces at Canyon de Chelly that allowed the military to build minimal forts and trading posts on Navajo land in exchange for various gifts and annual payments. In 1851, the government built Fort Defiance at the center of Navajo lands, which became the central command center for US forces in the Southwest. Later, the government built Fort Wingate, then constructed more settlements, and increased its military presence on Navajo lands, reducing their lands and breaking the treaty. This greatly upset the Navajo. In 1860, Navajo warriors attacked Fort Defiance, primarily because settlers' livestock was destroying their grazing lands. The attack was unsuccessful, and the Navajo lost more of their lands. During this time, the government forced the Navajo to learn to speak English and other American customs.

During the outbreak of the Civil War, the American military abandoned Fort Defiance and went to Texas with all the troops needed for the war. The Navajo, sensing an opportunity, increased their raids on the settlers in the region, aiming to drive them away and reclaim Navajo lands. These actions did not sit well with the American Government. The US military planned a swift response, one that would demoralize the Navajos.

After defeating Confederate forces from Texas, the US military returned to the region and appointed Lieutenant Colonel Kit Carson to carry out its response. Since he had been a valuable leader in defeating the Confederates, he was trusted to complete this operation. Carson's troops executed the planned response by systematically burning Navajo villages, crops, property, and hogans. Because of this, the Navajo had to eventually surrender due to food and housing shortages. They were forced to travel by foot to a reservation in the New Mexico Territory: a 300-mile walk that took at least 18 days, with hundreds of Navajo dying on the way—this later came to be infamously known as "The Long Walk." The Navajo's way of life was thus horribly disrupted due to the success of the US military response. Living under this duress, they could not be at peace with their spiritual world. Over time, they slowly adjusted to these changes, coming to peace with the situation.

The Navajo, like other Indian tribes, believed in living peacefully with nature and had strong spiritual connections. According to their core belief, maintaining a balance between mind, body, and spirit was necessary to achieving peace with the spiritual world. Chief Lonewolf longed for the Navajo to do this while they were on Earth. He knew the Navajo would lose all sense of peace if they gave more land away.

As a young boy, he had wandered the Navajo lands by himself. He did this so often that people knew he was a loner. He desired to get closer to all the things that surrounded him. As a teenager, he hunted and killed a wolf that threatened the Navajo and earned the name Lonewolf. He grew up to become a respected person in the tribe and soon became their chief. He aimed to always protect the Navajo and their land. This, he believed, would complete their life balance, ensuring a connection to the spiritual world.

Chief Lonewolf and his people were riding in a burial tribute to honor a fallen Navajo warrior, Aharon. He had been fatally injured by a bear while hunting. A tribute ride was a high honor given to people of respect and character who sacrificed for the Navajo. He was a friend of Two-Rivers.

As a child, Two-Rivers had a talent for fishing. According to the elders, he caught enough fish for two rivers, despite there being only one: hence his name. Two-Rivers was six feet tall, which made him taller than most Navajos. He was muscular, with long black hair that he kept tied up. He was close friends with Chief Lonewolf's daughter, Nizhoni, who was also friends with Aharon. Nizhoni was a beautiful eighteen-year-old with long black hair and flawless skin. She was given the name Nizhoni because it meant "beautiful." She loved running in the field where the Navajo tribe gathered crops. The first time Two-Rivers started having feelings for her was when he spotted her running through a field. Aharon knew how much they cared for each other. He was the reason they started courting one another. They were both saddened by their friend's death, but they knew his spirit had passed onto the next world, and that comforted them. On this ride, they were with Chief Lonewolf.

"Aharon would appreciate all the riders," Two-Rivers said.

"Yes, he was close to many of them," Nizhoni replied.

"The bear that killed him took a good Navajo from this world." Two-Rivers said.

"Many years ago, we had bears and wolves kill some of our people," Chief Lonewolf said. "In those days we lost many good Navajo, lost a lot of bears and wolves too."

"These animals are dangerous, but serve a purpose," Two-Rivers replied.

"What purpose do those killers serve?" Nizhoni said, still upset over Aharon's death.

"They are killers of deer on our lands and the hogs the Spanish left," Two-Rivers replied. "Those animals produce babies fast, then eat our crops, which limits our food."

The ride continued in silence for a moment. Chief Lonewolf was about to speak of the circle all life plays for one another when Nizhoni said, "The spirits make sure all life plays an equal role with each other. I just wish Aharon was here to experience more life with us." She was growing in her understanding of their ways, and this made Chief Lonewolf proud of her; it made him even more driven to ensure that the Navajo land remained.

"That is correct, my daughter. As we come from the ground, so we will return," Chief Lonewolf replied. "Then these animals feed on the grass from us, then we feed on them. Everything has its purpose in life."

Chief Lonewolf was proud of his daughter for following the Navajo tradition and, even though she was grieving, she still took part in this ride. He wanted a better future for his daughter—a peaceful future with the rest of the Navajos, with a focus on their spirituality. He wanted her, and her children after her, to run freely on their land without worrying about outside threats—he did not want railroads through their sacred land.

But little did he know of the devious plan the Baron and Dane were crafting in response to his refusal to sell their land.

Eight

Barbed Wire Prairie

The 1880s were not kind to the cowboy way of life. Work was hard to find; gone were the days of free-roaming cowboys traveling through the southwestern landscape; and now, they had to work for others for survival.

The southwestern landscape has sweeping beauty from the desert plains to the stunning mountain ranges. The open ranges are sprawling and allow people to travel for days without coming across another human being. A wandering coyote or a group of antelope racing across the landscape could be the only visitors to cross a traveler's path. A cowboy could ride on seemingly endless plains, then one would see a mountain peak on the horizon that grows by the minute during an approach. As westward expansion picked up steam, this open landscape became smaller with the creation of ranches. Cowboys needed to survive and had to look for work on these newly created ranches.

Oscar, Boyd, and Ben teamed up to seek ranch jobs. The three of them worked well together since they had been friends since 1882.

"What is the name of the next ranch?" Ben asked.

"It is the Log Cabin Ranch, owned by Gaylon Townsend," Boyd replied.

"I assumed most cabins were built from logs, at least in Texas they are," Oscar replied.

"We use grass and yucca to make our wickiups. They're easier to move than log cabins," Ben said with a grin on his face. He still did not understand the white people's need to be settled in one place. The Apache purposely selected shelters that allowed for quick assembly and disassembly.

"In Texas, we only use grass and sticks to burn in fire pits, so we can cook barbacoa," Oscar said. "If we get this ranching job, I will cook us some."

"That sounds like a name for a snake," Boyd replied as he and Ben laughed at their friend's suggestion that they try this Texan dish. These two Cowboys had ridden together for a while now. Their friendship had grown with their adventures.

Boyd and Ben met in 1878 when Ben joined the Lincoln County Regulators. The Lincoln County Regulators convinced Ben to join them despite his loyalty to the Apache. The US Cavalry had rounded the Apache up and forced them onto the reservations. He refused to go to a reservation and roamed solo until 1878 when he went to Lincoln County. In those early days, he became good friends with John Rose and learned how to be part of a team.

"Laugh about barbacoa. One day all of America will eat it," Oscar said with the utmost sincerity. Even though he lived in the New Mexico Territory, he still considers himself a Texan.

Oscar grew up in South Texas, near Brownsville. His family fought for Texan independence against Santa Anna and the United States during the Mexican–American War. His family were proud Americans and were happy to be part of Texan history. Oscar left home seeking adventure. In 1882, he met the American Cowboys and quickly became friends with them. After winning a shooting contest against Boyd, which earned him respect from Frank and John, he joined the group. Soon, he became good friends with Michael. In his grieving, he did not blame Boyd for Michael's death as Frank did. He just hoped for a chance to have vengeance on the man who murdered his friend. That man was Dane.

Boyd, besides losing Frank's trust, was also distraught over losing Michael. He had met Frank in 1871 while working as security for the Union Pacific Railroad—a difficult situation for Boyd, as he was a former Confederate soldier and John and Frank were Union soldiers. He had to work hard to gain their trust. Frank could not understand how he could fight for the Confederacy, but Boyd had cogent reasons. According to him, the federal government could not tell individual states what to do. He was against slavery, but he didn't want the federal government to interfere with state autonomy. For Frank, the war had nothing to do with the states' rights—it was all about freedom for his people. Boyd's family had no connections to slave owners. They were poor and had to fight for survival. He continued that fight when enlisting with the Confederacy as an act of loyalty to the US Constitution's tenth amendment. Once Boyd left home to fight in the war, he never saw his family again. Returning to visit them in late 1864, he discovered they had all perished in a fire. His family had lived in Rome, Georgia, and were victims of Union General William Sherman's cruel tactics of burning southern cities so the Confederacy could not return for supplies. He blamed himself for not being there for them. Devastated, he leaned on the men around him during the war for support. Once the war was over, Boyd, like most of the country, was ready to move on with his life. Finding Frank and John helped him to establish a close atmosphere with their group. Boyd knew it would take a while for him to earn Frank's trust. It was only much later, in Texas, after the Cowboys, who had finished their work at Union Pacific Railroad, were hired by the Red River Railway, that Boyd fully gained Frank and John's trust when confronting the notorious Bell gang. Afterward, their friendship solidified, and in 1873, Frank and John asked Boyd to join the Lincoln County Regulators with them.

At present, everything seemed lost for Boyd. And, once again, he felt like he could not stop a tragedy from happening. First his family's death in Georgia, and now Michael's death. Thoughts that he failed people close to him haunted Boyd. He was desperate to make amends with those thoughts. These men were now his family. He did not want to lose that again. But, in the meantime, the Cowboys needed money, and they had to find work.

They found work along the "barbed wire prairie"—the name cowboys gave to the land they used to roam. With the United States expanding westward, the Indians were not the only group who had lost their way of life. Ranching and over-expansion led to the 1886 barbed wire fence explosion across the Southwest. There were restrictions on where the cowboys could ride and even camp. To make matters worse, in 1886 and 1887, a terribly dry summer and a vicious winter followed. The barbed wire prairie made a cowboy's life, which had always been difficult, worse, forcing most cowboys to look for jobs as ranch hands, tending to sick cattle, or working on fences. Eventually, these cowboy jobs dried up from Texas to Kansas, causing them to become unwanted and unnecessary to most.

This had become the life of a cowboy. Now, if the barbed wire didn't stop them, the harshness of the growing new world did. By 1890, they were left to search for their place in this new world—a significant fall for these proud wranglers. They often worked 18-hour days in rain, snow, daylight, or darkness. They rarely fought Indians anymore and usually worked multiple ranch jobs a year just to make ends meet. Most of them had small to medium body frames, and their lifestyle made it difficult to maintain good health.

Despite the struggle of maintaining the cowboy lifestyle, most of them, including Boyd, Oscar, and Ben, were not ready to trade it for anything. To avoid moving to towns for work, they needed a job that allowed them to continue living their dream as cowboys.

As the Cowboys rode through the gates of the Log Cabin Ranch, Oscar said, "I cannot believe my eyes. There is a log cabin on this ranch." Which enlisted laughter from the other travelers.

"Maybe there will be cattle on this ranch. Weird not to put that in the ranch's name," Ben replied, resulting in more laughter from the men.

As they continued down the path to the cabin, Boyd became preoccupied with other things on his mind. He was concerned about the future of the American Cowboys. They had helped so many people; they meant a lot to people in need. He cast his mind back to the days when he'd worked along with Frank and John for the Red River Railway.

Nine

Red River Railway

1872

The Texas heat was brutal.

One begged for nighttime to come and cool it down. But the relief was short-lived: a couple of hours after sunrise, the temperature would rise to one hundred degrees. Frank, John, and Boyd were in Sherman, Texas, working for the Red River Railway. The humidity in Sherman worsened the heat. The only thing hotter than the Texas heat was the chili served by Skip, the company man hired by the railway to feed everyone. The chili was hot but delicious. Eating it was the favorite part for the guys who worked for the Red River Railway.

"Skip, did you only put jalapenos in this chili? My mouth is on fire!" Boyd said.

"You don't like it, don't eat it," Skip replied with a scowl on his face. Skip was not known for having a pleasant personality, but he made up for it with his good food.

Boyd, grinning at Skip, replied, "Well, I have to eat. I don't want to be the only one here without a burnt tongue. That wouldn't be fair."

"Go sit down and leave me be, there's too much work to be gabbing."

Boyd laughed, then started walking toward the table so he could eat with Frank and John.

The Cowboys had been working together and providing security for the railways since the Civil War, and this food was the best. Getting a good meal helped the Cowboys after a hard day's work on the railway. Mealtime for the three Cowboys helped ease tension because it helped to build camaraderie between them from their challenging situation because of their differing backgrounds during the Civil War. They had reluctantly gone to work for the Red River Railway as a group because of this and were still working through those feelings.

"Hey fellas, how's the chili today, hot or fire?" Boyd asked as he sat down at the table.

Frank nodded his head, then said, "Somewhere in between, but closer to hot."

"There is nothing better than Skip's hot chili, as long as there's a watering hole nearby to put out the flames," John replied, which caused the Cowboys to laugh.

"If you don't watch your tongue, I'll put you in that watering hole," Skip replied from the food wagon.

"Easy Skip. If we're gone, who is going to eat your cooking?" Frank retorted. The Cowboys laughed again, which enlisted a smile from the old cook. Frank enjoyed this group of Cowboys, even with their challenges.

He'd been tempted to leave Texas occasionally, but he ended up staying. If Maybelle hadn't been sick, he would've tried to move back toward Mississippi. But once she succumbed to yellow fever, he realized the importance of staying in Texas, since Jane took care of Michael. Unless a better offer came along, it seemed risky to leave a guaranteed job.

The situation was hard for Boyd as well. He sometimes felt out of place with their differing backgrounds. He was, like everyone, just trying to put his life back together after the devastating war.

That is where the railway came into play. It offered security jobs for former soldiers, and it seemed to assure them of a profitable life. Frank and John thought the same, and they all ended up at Union Pacific Railroad by chance. It helped that Frank and John had experienced railway security at Brice's Cross Road. That experience helped push them into this industry. The railway assigned them together because they were the best.

It was only after working together for a while with the Union Pacific Railway that they discovered Boyd's past. The Cowboys faced many challenging days trying to overcome their pasts, but they persevered. They went to work for the Red River Railway in 1871 after the Union Pacific Railway started using the US Cavalry as security. They became the best at boarding hijacked trains, and the railway used them as their primary team. It required great skill and was very difficult to accomplish. They had to ride up to a moving train, board it without getting shot, make their way to the engine room, and retake the train. If there was valuable cargo, they had to secure that cargo at the same time. Many men who tried this job did not live to talk about it. But Frank, John, and Boyd not only lived to talk about it—they also did it better than anyone else.

A brooding man with red hair walked by Skip's food wagon and looked across the food tables. Seeing Frank, John, and Boyd, he smirked and then started walking toward their table. It was the railways' foreman, Danny, who gave work assignments to the men. He and Frank didn't care for one another. His smirk was for Frank.

"We have a job for you boys," Danny said to the men once he reached their table.

"If the job is for boys, why don't you do it?" Frank replied.

Danny had a knack for talking down to the Cowboys, and Frank wasn't pleased about that. A year earlier, they had had a tense conversation that resulted in a fistfight. Danny was on the losing end of the fight. That made him a bit more respectful.

Looking at Frank, he calmly replied, "Gentlemen, the company has a job for you."

"Much better. Now it sounds like you might need us."

Boyd smiled at this interaction. He, like the other Cowboys, appreciated Frank speaking up for them. The foreman had not earned their respect since he never worked with them. They sure would not give him respect in return. In Texas, a man earned his respect.

"What's the job, Danny?" John said. He was hoping to move the conversation along so they could finish their chili. He knew it would be a challenging job since they were the best.

"We need you all to board a train hijacked by the Bell gang."

All the Cowboys looked at each other with this news. The Bell gang were notorious train-robbing bandits that killed anyone who got in their way. Their main trademark was to kill the train conductor and set him ablaze as a warning to anyone who might try to stop them.

"Say no more Danny, we will take care of it," John said. The Bell gang needed to be brought to justice. This would be their opportunity to do just that. The Cowboys finished their chili, then got up and headed off to plan the train rescue.

"Thanks for the chili, Skip. Next time it would be quicker if you just lit my mouth on fire," Boyd said while passing the cook on his way out.

"How about I punch you in the mouth?" Skip replied with a devious grin toward the cowboy. The Cowboys laughed at this and tipped their hats to Skip.

Frank and John had become fond of Boyd's sense of humor. They were getting to know one another, and their friendship was growing. They didn't choose to be working together initially but now couldn't imagine doing their jobs with anyone else.

They went to John's room and began mapping the route the hijacked train would travel, then found a location down that route to attempt the train rescue. The train had six cars, which included the engine, four passenger cars in the midsection, and a caboose. To get an idea of where the bandits were positioned on the train, the Cowboys would ride beside it. This mission would be at nighttime, to conceal their positions. Then, they would fall back to the caboose and board the train. Working together, they would systematically go through each train car, eliminating the bandits. Fortunately, there were no passengers on this train. Valuables were being moved by some local ranchers. They had hoped an empty train would not pique the interest of these bandits. They were wrong.

The Cowboys saddled up their horses and rode to the location they had mapped out to wait for the hijacked train. After a short time, John spotted the hijacked train and they prepared to start the rescue mission. By the time the train reached them, they needed their horses running at full speed or they would never board the train. The Cowboys' horses galloped their way toward the cut-off zone, which is where they needed to board the train. Horses were faster than trains; their top speed was around 30 miles an hour, whereas the trains typically ran at 18 miles an hour. But trains could go much further than tired horses. Now, with the horses running, they allowed the train engine to pass them while scouting through the train windows for the location of the bandits. They spotted two bandits in the engine, one in the third car, and the last two in the fourth car. They were ready to make their move and board the train.

They were lucky not to be spotted in the night's darkness. As the train pulled ahead of them, one by one they jumped onto the side of the train ladders on the caboose and boarded the train. These jumps toward a speeding train were very difficult, but the Cowboys were getting more skilled at it with every rescue. John was no longer nervous when boarding a moving train. He was proud that his skills at this were as good as Brody's.

Once they were all in the caboose, John called them together and said, "Thomas is in the engine. We must be quiet working our way to him."

"Try not to use your guns," Frank replied.

"What are we supposed to do, hit them with our cowboy hats?" Boyd said, which made John chuckle.

Frank was not one to joke in a serious setting and gave Boyd a perturbed look.

"Choke them out if you can. That will be nice and quiet," John said.

The Cowboys nodded in agreement, then started making their way through the train cars.

The Bell gang comprised five outlaws, most of them unknown except for their leader, Thomas Bell, the notoriously brutal Confederate Lieutenant to Dane during the Civil War. Boyd despised Thomas and knew he was evil. But they questioned whether Boyd would be more loyal to a former Confederate or them. They would soon find out.

The first passenger car was still empty. They had achieved the element of surprise. Slowly, they positioned themselves near the fourth train car door. They would have to be decisive to take care of the first two outlaws they encountered. The bandits were focused on searching for valuables and were distracted. Boyd and Frank snuck up behind them and each choked the bandits until they were unconscious.

The men worked their way through to the third train car. John snuck up behind the preoccupied bandit and choked the third outlaw out. This left the last two bandits in the engine compartment, including Thomas. The men made their way through the second train car and positioned themselves near the door. They were ready to take Thomas and regain control of the train.

"John, take the outside of the train on the right. Boyd, take the outside of the train on the left. I will give the sign for us to ambush them on three sides." They all moved into position. Frank was about to pounce.

But unbeknownst to the Cowboys, the railroad company, in a preemptive act to stop the hijacked train, had placed logs across the tracks. They did this to make sure that these bandits were stopped.

Thomas and his remaining partner failed to see the logs until the last minute and had to grab onto the engine compartment side rails for support, preparing for the train to smash into the logs.

Upon impact, Frank was thrown into the engine compartment, and his Colt Peacemaker was lost. The outlaws quickly jumped on Frank and held him up. On the right side of the engine, the crash had almost knocked John down onto the wheels. Though he steadied himself, he could not get into a position to get into the engine room. This only left Boyd, who was holding onto the side ladder on the left side of the train. Fortunately, he had not fallen when the train smashed into the logs. If the logs had knocked the train off its tracks, everyone could have died.

Boyd could see into the engine room. Frank was about to be shot by Thomas. Boyd quickly aimed his Winchester rifle and, with two shots, killed Thomas and his partner. Frank fell to his knees, and the outlaws fell to the ground. When Frank looked up, he was stunned to see Boyd standing there with his Winchester rifle and Thomas's dead body on the engine floor. By now, John had made his way into the engine room and saw that Boyd had saved Frank's life.

Frank quoted Proverbs 3:5, *"Trust in the Lord with all your heart and do not lean on your understanding,"* and told Boyd, "I don't understand your past, but I trust God knows more than me. Thank you."

Nodding at Frank in agreement, Boyd said, "We are a team, and you can always trust me." Frank smiled at Boyd, got up off the train floor, went to Boyd, and shook his hand.

"We're not just a team, we are friends."

It thrilled John to see the Cowboys coming together. They couldn't control their pasts, but they could determine their futures. He felt that their future together would be good.

With the train secured, the Cowboys returned to the base camp in Sherman. They were upset with the Red River Railway for not trusting them to complete their job and leaving logs on the train tracks—that had almost cost Frank his life. So, they actively talked about looking for a new job. Little did they know then that there was an opening coming their way in the New Mexico Territory.

A rancher from Lincoln County, Don Jennings, was waiting for John at the railway station with an excellent job offer.

"Excuse me, are you John Rose?" Don asked a suspicious John, who was on his way to Danny's office to let him know the Cowboys were not happy with the company's decision to crash the train.

Cautiously, John replied, "Who wants to know, friend?"

"I'm Don Jennings from Lincoln County in the New Mexico Territory. I come on behalf of our county to offer a job. We need help to protect ranches and defend the people in the county from bandits. You come highly recommended by Brody Sammons."

John had not heard Brody's name in quite some time. He knew he was still in the US Army and rode with the Cavalry.

"Brody is a good man and great friend. If he sent you, then we are off to a good start."

"That is good to hear, Mr. Rose. I have always prided myself on having a good name. That is the only thing people cannot take away from you."

"Call me John, my friend. How do you know Brody?"

"Brody and his Cavalry regiment came through Lincoln County on their way to Fort Sumner. When I told him about our problems, he suggested coming to find you."

'Why didn't the Cavalry get involved and help you with your problem?"

"That's the problem. The local sheriff is on the wrong side of this issue for us ranchers. The Cavalry doesn't like to get involved with local jurisdiction issues."

"The sheriff is on the side of the bandits?" John replied.

"Unfortunately, they are working together. The Justice of the Peace will help us, but he needs men. That's where you come in."

After pondering the situation momentarily, John responded, "Let me hear more about this job in Lincoln County. I think you have found your man."

"I think you will like our offer. May we sit and talk?"

The two men found a table inside the railway station to discuss the offer. The offer was for John to put together some of the Cowboys, and then the Justice of the Peace would deputize them to "regulate" theft from their ranches. This intrigued John, and he felt it could be the next move for the Cowboys. He thanked Don and promised to be in touch soon. He received information from the rancher that he had two days to decide. That's when his train would leave Sherman.

John went to Frank's cabin to discuss the Lincoln County job. Frank was playing with Michael. John was more interested in his nanny, Jane. She had been close to Frank's wife for years, and she had stayed around to be Michael's nanny after Maybelle's death. Frank needed help since he was working for the railway. She was as loyal to the Morgans as they were to her. Jane made eye contact with John, and both felt strongly for each other. Her eyes were what he noticed first. They were mesmerizing. She slowly moved her hair over her right ear with her hand. John knew this was the best, and possibly the last, chance he would have to ask her to accompany him for dinner.

Frank interrupted their stare when he asked, "John, what do you need?"

Reluctantly taking his eyes from Jane, he said, "I think we have a job offer in Lincoln County in the New Mexico Territory."

"That is good news. After today, it's time for us to move on."

Jane became worried that if John left, she could miss her opportunity to get to know him better. She wanted to at least have the chance to get to know him. She could not wait for the details and asked, "What is the job offer?"

Frank and John looked over at Jane, surprised she was interested in this business.

"Some ranchers need help protecting their property and want us Cowboys to fill that role," John said, then smiled at Jane.

"We are going to move, daddy?" Michael inquisitively asked.

As the room became silent, and with everyone looking at Frank, he said, "I think we might move, son."

John, Jane, and Frank all looked at each other and smiled. They were all ready for a change. John and Jane were relieved they would stay together.

Then, with a surprise to John, Frank said, "Invite Boyd to go with us."

This pleased him, as this showed how far Boyd and Frank's relationship had improved.

"I will go tell him now. We can meet up shortly and discuss."

On his way out of the room, John looked at Jane and they smiled at each other. This gave him the confidence he needed to ask Jane to dinner. Then he noticed a paper on Frank's wall behind Jane. It mentioned the Red River Railway summer dance. He knew this could be the perfect opportunity to spend time with the woman who had caught his eye.

He looked back at Jane and said, "Would you do me the pleasure and attend the dance with me?"

She looked at John and then Frank and said, "Yes."

Trying to contain his excitement, he said, "Great, I will come to get you at seven."

Jane nodded at John, then went chasing after Michael, who ran into the larger room.

Frank, who had a smile on his face, said, "Good job, buddy. Now, who is going to teach you to dance?"

Not wanting to miss an opportunity to be with Jane, John had forgotten about one issue with the dance: he didn't know how to dance.

Turning to leave the room, John said, "We will figure that out later. I had to take my shot." All he cared about was getting to spend time with the woman he yearned for.

That would be at the Red River Railway summer dance.

Ten

The Dance

John was nervous.

Jane had agreed to go with him to the dance. He had long desired a chance to spend time with this beautiful woman who had captured his attention. Fortunately, Boyd was an excellent dancer and agreed to give John a quick lesson. But first, business needed to be addressed with the upcoming move.

"We need to take the Goodnight–Loving Trail to the New Mexico Territory," John said.

"That will be tough. We will have to travel through Indian territory by Horsehead Crossing," Frank replied.

"Most of the Indians have been moved out of Texas and into reservations in the New Mexico Territory. Maybe that won't be an issue," Boyd said.

"Small groups of Indians or bandits will be too much for our small travel group to handle," Frank said.

John knew there was difficulty traveling north from Texas. There were few choices, and they all came with risks. "I think our small group will be beneficial. Large groups attract attention from nefarious groups. I think we'll be safe if we're smart," John said.

After a brief pause, Frank said, "That's a good observation. If there are no disagreements, then we'll ride for the Goodnight–Loving Trail and then north to Lincoln County."

The Cowboys all agreed to the plan. Their destiny now awaited them in the New Mexico Territory.

"John, are you ready to learn to dance?" Boyd said, changing the conversation toward the evening's dance.

"Ready as I will ever be. Just be kind to me," John replied.

He got out of his chair and went to Boyd for his lesson. John easily caught on to how to dance to a slow tune. However, he also needed to know how to square dance. Boyd attempted to explain and then show John how to square dance. It turned out he was not skilled with his feet. His unique dance style soon had the Cowboys laughing.

Boyd said, "John, you look like a chicken pecking at worms. Relax your shoulders."

"I am relaxed. What is wrong with this dance?" John asked.

"Nothing if you are a chicken eating," Frank replied, enlisted a laugh from Boyd.

"You know what, I think this dance style is just fine," John replied.

Boyd, finally giving up trying to teach John to dance, said, "I think we've taught you as much as we can. How about you just stay sitting in a chair and stick to slow tunes?" The Cowboys all laughed and headed out to get dressed for the dance. John enjoyed time with his friends and could appreciate a little ribbing from them—he would be the first to rib them if they were in his place. However, nothing bothered him as he prepared to go on his date with Jane. From the first time he saw her, he felt she would be his wife, that they were meant to be together. He would endure whatever was necessary just to get close to her, and he hoped that this dance could be the opportunity for her to fall in love with him.

Little did John know that Jane had similar feelings for him. The first time he walked into the Morgans' cabin years earlier, she knew they would fall in love. Now, sitting in front of her mirror at home and doing her makeup, she was so nervous about the dance that night. She wanted to get closer to him. Unlike John, she was a skilled dancer, and she couldn't wait to be on the dance floor with him—not because of his skills, but just to be with him. She was very excited when he asked her to go to the dance. Despite her efforts to conceal her emotions, she seemed to have given them away. She didn't want to come across as overly interested and scare him away —she didn't want to do anything that would jeopardize their being together. But she was finding it difficult not to appear eager.

There was a knock at the door, and John announced himself. It was time to go. Jane was very nervous. She powdered her face one more time and then opened the door. Once their eyes met, they blushed. They were both meant to be together, and they had this night on the dance floor to discover that.

Soon after, they entered the dance hall at the Red River Railway Station and awkwardly found some seats. The band was playing square-dance music. Four band members were individually playing a fiddle, a guitar, a banjo, and a mandolin. It was a festive scene inside the dance hall. The dance floor was full of couples square dancing. After surveying the room, John knew he was not nearly ready to square dance. Now, even his chicken-pecking dance moves seemed incorrect to him.

Jane was so nervous she could hardly look at John, but he took this as a sign that she was not interested in him. To pique her interest, he said, "So, what's your favorite type of train?" He immediately regretted saying this; it embarrassed him to even pose such a silly question to a beautiful woman.

Jane awkwardly replied, "I think the kind here is okay. Have you been on a lot of trains?"

"Oh yes, I've been on many trains and such." Once again, he regretted his words and shook his head.

Noticing that she was avoiding eye contact with him, he wondered whether she was bored with him.

At the same moment, Jane hoped John was interested in her, but she was worried because he seemed indifferent.

Watching this debacle unfold from their seats, Frank and Boyd were laughing. Frank finally got up. "Those two need a push or they're never going to leave those seats."

Boyd laughed as Frank headed over to John and Jane's table. "That's what I told him to do, remember?" Boyd said.

He smiled at Boyd and left. When he reached John and Jane's table, he said, "The railway station makes a great dance hall, doesn't it?"

John and Jane both agreed, nodding their heads, but neither of them looked at him.

"The band is playing good music tonight," Frank said.

Once again, they only nodded their heads.

Frank turned and looked at Boyd, who shrugged his shoulders, still laughing. Frank turned back to the table. "John, if you don't go dance with Jane, I will."

John and Jane looked at Frank, who was staring back at them. John turned to Jane and, with a tremor in voice, said, "Jane, may I have this dance?"

"Yes, you may have this dance," Jane replied.

John took her by the hand and walked toward the dance floor. Jane elbowed Frank on the way, and he laughed. Fortunately for John, the band changed from playing square dance music to a slow tune led by the violinists. He was greatly relieved. Slow dancing was more his speed. Stepping onto the dance floor, John and Jane were nervous. With the violinists playing the slow song, John placed a hand on Jane's hip and grabbed her hand with his other hand. They smiled, looking into each other's eyes. John tried to remember what Boyd had taught him earlier that day, and Jane was trying not to show him how much she liked him.

Suddenly, the band picked up the tempo and began playing another square dance tune. Terrified of this musical change, John looked over to the band and saw Boyd standing near them, encouraging them to change to a fast tune. Boyd couldn't help but laugh, he was enjoying giving his friend a hard time. Then he held up a finger to John. Turning to the band, Boyd reached into his pants pocket and pulled out some money. He then reached it out to the violinist, who happily took the money, said something to his fellow band members, and then returned to the slow ballad.

"What is the band doing?" Jane asked. "That was strange."

"I think they have a new director who needs to sit down."

Jane looked over to see Boyd laughing near the band. She grinned and shook her head.

They slowly began dancing around the dance floor, and eventually, their nerves settled and they relaxed in each other's arms. As the song took them from one area of the dance floor to another, they locked eyes with each other. John's heart was beating incredibly fast; he never thought he would be this much in love. The earlier dance lesson from Boyd helped John to dance to this slow tune. Jane's expertise in dancing was also beneficial. He marveled at Jane's stunning green eyes and her flowing blonde hair. Everything about her was perfect in his eyes, and he never wanted to let her go. Jane's nerves subsided, as everything felt right. John's arms were powerful, and his green eyes fascinated her. She had hoped to be in love one day, and she had been searching for the right person. Slowly, one step at a time, they fell in love on the dance floor, ready for their forever to begin. John slowly leaned in to kiss Jane, and she moved toward him. As their lips touched, they lost themselves in one another, and everything else disappeared.

The song continued to play, and they stood still, lost in their first kiss.

Frank smiled. His thoughts went to Maybelle. He longed for her every day. He prayed that John and Jane would have a never-ending love. The only thing harder than finding the person you are meant to be with is having to say goodbye to them. But tonight was about new love. Tonight was about John and Jane.

Tomorrow, they would plan for the Goodnight–Loving Trail.

Eleven

Goodnight-Loving

In 1866, cattlemen Charles Goodnight and Oliver Loving, hoping to gain business, drove their Texas longhorns northbound. They would start in Texas and end in Colorado. Their journey began by using the old Butterfield-Overland Mail route, going through central Texas to Horsehead Crossing then following the Pecos River north into Fort Sumner, located in the New Mexico Territory, and concluding in Denver, Colorado. The cattlemen hoped the increase in settlers, soldiers at military outposts, and Navajo on reservations, would be a profitable venture. Their hopes of turning a profit came harder than expected and with substantial costs. The biggest was in 1867 when Loving died after being attacked by Comanches. Goodnight would persevere and grow his cattle business by extending the cattle drive into Wyoming. The path they took created the Goodnight–Loving Trail, which became one of the most traveled during the late 1800s.

John, Frank, and Boyd decided to use the Goodnight–Loving Trail when moving to Lincoln County. When they informed Red River Railway, they were not pleased. They also did not have a say in the matter. The Cowboys had lost their trust in the company. Now, the only option was to part ways. In short order, the Cowboys loaded two wagons and began the journey to the New Mexico Territory. John eagerly volunteered, which was no surprise to Frank, to drive a wagon with Jane. Boyd and Frank would manage the other wagon while rotating as the rider on horseback. It was common practice to have at least one rider on horseback to scout the upcoming area for bandits or Indians. Michael would rotate riding in the two wagons. The trail from Sherman took the group to Fort Worth, down to Fort Concho, then over to Horsehead Crossing. From there, it would be a northern push following the Pecos River to their new home. Their travels were without incident and they quickly made their way to Horsehead Crossing.

"Why is this called Horsehead?" Michael asked.

Pondering the same thing, Jane replied, "Maybe a horse lives here, but you can only see the head?" This caused Michael to laugh. He was a happy four-year-old boy, and Jane loved to make him laugh.

With little thought of the company on the wagon, John said, "You see those skulls on the dirt bank to the right? That's a horse's skull left by Comanches marking this spot." This caused Jane and Michael to look at him with expressions of shock. The thought of Indians in this country put fear into most, especially women and the young. Knowing he had spooked his travel companions, especially the woman he was courting, caused him to change his phrasing. "What I mean is pioneers left rocks that look like a horsehead for others to follow." This caused Jane and Michael to relax and even smile.

"John, you are funny," Michael replied. "Those rocks don't look like horses. They have no ears." Jane and Michael laughed at this and nudged John on his right arm. He smiled at this response since his earlier comment had scared them.

John looked over at Michael and said, "You know what horses like to chew on? Little boys' ears." He then made his hand into a pretend horse, placed it near Michael's ear, and pretended it was a horse nibbling on it. They all laughed at his joke.

Jane took John's hand and said, "Okay, that horse has had plenty of ears for today. He needs to sleep it off now." As she moved his hand down, she tightened her grip gently, looked at John, and smiled. He immediately blushed and returned the smile. His love for this woman had only grown since leaving Sherman. She was equally enchanted with him.

"Why are you turning so red, John?" Michael asked.

"Because I am a happy cowboy," John replied.

"That's funny. I don't turn red when I'm happy," Michael replied. "You sure it isn't from eating my ear?" This caused them to laugh again. Their trip was going well, and they enjoyed Michael's company. It made them both start wanting a child of their own.

Looking around the landscape, Jane said, "This land is so flat and barren."

She was accurate in her statement. The area was in the middle of West Texas. Other than the Pecos River, which they were near, it was also dry, primarily because it was located in the Chihuahua Desert. The climate did not seem as bad as Sherman's, though, thanks to the low humidity. As far as they could see, the landscape was brown and yellow. Occasionally, a tumbleweed would roll across the ground as if being chased by a coyote. Instead of a pursuit, the tumbleweed was being pushed by the powerful wind gusts. The heat, however, was nothing compared to the brutal dust storms that would appear out of nowhere. The sight of approaching dark brown clouds of dust was the only warning that one was coming. When seeing these, travelers would have to hunker down with face coverings until it passed. Much of the landscape was dirt, mesquite bushes, and dead brush. It was a welcome sight for the group when they made it to the Pecos River. Finally, there was something green in the landscape. They had not seen fresh water for many miles. They desperately needed this water for the remainder of their journey.

The wagons came to a stop near the river and the travelers dismounted to start preparing to cross. There was more than one reason for traveling the Goodnight–Loving Trail. It was a well-established route, crossed the Pecos River, which provided travelers with fresh water, and had a low crossing spot on the river. The plan was for the group to cross the river, camp for the night, then head north for Lincoln County in the morning. The group went to the river and began filling up their canteens.

"Daddy is here!" Michael exclaimed, running over to his father, who had ridden up on his horse. He quickly dismounted the horse just in time to scoop Michael up and give him a big hug.

"How is my boy doing?" Frank replied. "Did you behave in the wagon?"

"Yes, Daddy I did. John even showed me some skulls the Comanche left." Frank glanced at John with a stern look.

"Those were pioneers, Michael, remember?" Jane said, trying to help John. Frank's look quickly turned into a smile. He smiled back at him and laughed.

"We had a fun ride with your boy. He is a blessing," John said while turning his head toward Jane. "I hope to have my own someday." Jane began blushing and smiled at John.

"Look Daddy, now Jane is turning red, just like John did on the wagon. She must be happy, too." Frank began shaking his head while looking at the couple.

Boyd had just finished filling his canteens and let out a loud laugh and said, "You two need your own wagon."

"Tomorrow, Michael can ride with me so these two can be happy all to themselves," Frank replied.

Boyd could sense the couple was embarrassed and, in true form to himself, added to their predicament by saying, "Well Frank, if they are left alone, we may lose the wagon." John and Jane were less impressed.

"How about we just get the wagons ready to cross the river?" John replied.

"That sounds like a good idea. If everyone wants to eat tonight," Jane said, implying she would not cook for the men afterward if this joking continued. She and John looked at one another and smiled. They felt what everyone could see. They were in love.

They all worked together to prepare the wagons and move them across the river. Frank was sure to keep Michael with him. Any time danger was present, his son stayed with him. Jane cooked dinner while the others prepared the wagons for the journey north. Soon they were all sitting down around a campfire and enjoying a delicious stew after a hard journey. There was still a long way to go, but they had made significant progress. Boyd had slept a little first while the group was eating. He would be on the lookout for the night. Frank announced he was taking a sleeping Michael to bed. He picked up his son and carried him to the wagon.

Now alone, Jane and John went to the other wagon. They lay across its bench and looked up at the stars. The sky in West Texas was breathtaking. Stars went on for as far as one could see. The warm breeze felt wonderful blowing across their faces. As they gazed into the night sky, neither wanted this moment to end. Being together was what they had both dreamed of. Now that dream was a reality. They hoped it was there forever.

"The stars are beautiful tonight," Jane said.

"Yes, but they are not the most beautiful thing I've seen tonight," John replied while looking toward Jane.

Jane grabbed his hand and held on to it. "Well, this sky is just amazing tonight, the best I have ever seen."

John replied, "The more complete your life is, the better the world around you looks."

Jane smiled and thought about how their relationship was going. She did not think her feelings for John could get any stronger after their first dance. She was wrong.

"John, what do you hope for once we get to Lincoln County?"

"I have always hoped for two things. With one of those now accomplished, all I need is the second."

After pausing for a moment, Jane finally said, "What is the second thing you have hoped for?" She was hoping he was going to say to marry her. She eagerly awaited his response.

"Well, I want a ranch. A big ranch surrounded by trees in the mountains and a family living a happy life." Jane's face dropped since he didn't mention her as his second hope. Sensing her disappointment with his response, he said, "Does that not sound good to you?"

"I was just hoping to be important in your future." After a brief pause, she said, "What was the thing you already accomplished?"

John looked at Jane, placed a hand on her cheek, and said, "Getting you to fall in love with me." Jane smiled at him. "You are my future, Jane. That's our family at the ranch." He rolled over toward Jane and slowly kissed her. Every time they kissed; he fell more in love. God was good, and Jane was the best gift He had given John. After their kiss, he reached into his pocket and pulled out a ring. He had purchased it in Fort Worth after their first dance. He would have married her then and there if he had built up the courage to ask her. The ring was a thin gold wedding band. He'd spent more than he wanted, but not enough for the love of his life.

Jane was speechless. She felt completely surprised. This is what she so badly wanted; she just didn't know he was there with her. As tears of joy filled her eyes, she couldn't imagine being happier.

With tears falling from his eyes, he said, "Jane, make me the happiest man and be my wife."

Jane slowly took the ring from him. It was the prettiest thing she had ever seen. Placing the ring on her finger, she said, "Yes, I will marry you!" They embraced and kissed again. Their hopes of never having their love end were being realized.

They both returned their gaze to the heavens above them, thankful they had each other and grateful to God for bringing them together. As they lay, shooting stars began streaming across the sky. The moment could not have been any better.

"Do you know why those stars shoot across the sky, Jane?" John asked.

Laughing, Jane said, "I guessed they were just falling."

Still looking at the sky, John said, "When someone dies, their spirit goes to the heavens and waits for their true love. Once their true love passes on, they go to the heavens to be reunited. The shooting star we see is them running to the true love that's been waiting for them." Jane smiled and squeezed John tighter.

"I like that better than them just falling. I hope you know my star has already run to you." The couple held one another long into the night, enjoying the blissfulness of their love.

They would make plans to marry in Lincoln County. The possibilities seemed endless with this new opportunity in the New Mexico Territory. Little did they know a war was coming to Lincoln County.

Twelve

Lincoln County War

1878

Ben Weathers was a proud member of the Apache tribe.

The Apache people were nomadic hunters and gatherers who roamed the Southwest. They were experts in warfare and highly skilled horsemen. The Apache women were known for their ability to find and prepare food from many plant sources. Ben's family had taught him these skills and taught him well. He had witnessed the US Cavalry forcing the Apache on long walks to the reservation forts as prisoners. In 1873, when his people were forced to go to the reservation, Ben refused to go; instead, he roamed solo and survived by relying on what he had learned from his people until he went to Lincoln County.

Ben had heard of the troubles that the people in Lincoln County were having with corrupt politicians and lawmen. He felt inclined to help them. It was especially important to Ben since Lincoln County was part of Apache land—it could be, he felt, his way of fighting against those who were doing wrong on Apache land.

He met John upon his arrival in Lincoln County and joined the Lincoln County Regulators. He felt secure being in this group because they were better equipped to fight against the corruption in Lincoln County. He decided that he would be a better asset for the Apache by fighting with the Regulators.

Ben respected John because he stood up for him if anyone questioned why an Apache was in the group. Frank and Boyd met Ben through John. Frank intrigued Ben, who had never seen a black man before. But he knew their struggles against the white man and immediately felt that bond with him.

Ben didn't know what to think of Boyd; he felt he was loud and full of himself. Boyd's sense of humor was lost on the Apache. However, what Ben liked about Boyd was that, like him, he carried a Winchester 1873 rifle. This rifle, of course, was to become known as "the gun that won the West." Both of them liked the idea of having fourteen rounds in the rifle and that it could use the same ammunition as their revolvers. This set them apart from John and Frank, who relied on their Colt Peacemakers. They quickly grew their friendship based on this choice in their firearms. They would go shooting together and became good friends from these moments.

Even though their choice of weapons was different, the group was stronger because of it. Having skilled riflemen was as important as having skilled cowboys who could wield handguns.

The Cowboys were excited about the opportunities the area offered them. Jane, though she worried about the conflicts, was happy here. She had married John in 1874, in a nice ceremony on Tunstall's ranch, and since her parents were deceased, Frank had given her away. While Frank and John worked, she took care of Michael. All the cowboys, including John and Jane, lived in separate houses on Tunstall's property, which made good sense, security-wise. Knowing Jane was with Michael also put Frank's mind at ease. He had worried that she wouldn't be able to care for Michael once she was married. Fortunately, that was not the case, and this was made possible because the Cowboys lived near each other and Jane had not gotten pregnant. She and John were discouraged that they had not been successful in having their own children. It did help raise her spirits by being close to Michael. This also helped Michael since she had been his mother figure since Maybelle's passing. She knew to be patient until God blessed her with a child.

The Lincoln County War disrupted the Cowboys' lives after they relocated there for Regulator jobs. The conflict began between two factions competing for profits from dry goods and cattle interests in the county. It started when Englishman John Tunstall challenged James Dolan in the dry goods trade. Lincoln County Sheriff William Brady allied with the Dolan faction and was aided by the Jesse Evans gang. This led Frank, John, Boyd, and Ben to help Tunstall's side. They utilized their roles as Lincoln County Regulators to help bring order to the area. The Cowboys rode as a separate faction of the main Lincoln County Regulators since none of them cared for their leader William Bonnie, who was also known as Billy the Kid. They considered him as no different from any other murdering outlaw. Unfortunately for the Regulators, Tunstall was murdered by Jesse Evans as the conflict was escalating. When Tunstall was murdered, they were made special constables to bring in Evans. The Cowboys vowed to bring Evans to justice for shooting Tunstall.

Lincoln County was beautiful, with green hills and large plains surrounded by high mountain ranges. In the mountains, one encountered large trees that went on for miles. While traveling through the mountains, a person felt serenity being out in this beautiful wilderness surrounded by these majestic trees. But this made the search for Evans even more difficult.

To prepare for their search for Evans, the Cowboys visited the trading post in Lincoln County for supplies. Once at the trading post, the owner, Cade, helped them get what they needed. He was a big man who was with an Apache woman named Vicki. Cade told them that she got her name from the woman Apache Chief Victorio. Cade was part of the Lincoln County Regulators, but only for supplies. Cade could not ride and shoot; he had injured his legs while riding a bull as a young man. Vicki, who was currently busy loading their wagon, prodded Cade to hurry with the supply list from the Cowboys. Cade quickly gathered the supplies and, once he was finished, pulled John and Frank aside.

"Guys, with Tunstall being killed, I'm no longer safe here with Vicki."

"We understand, Cade," John said. "Any ideas where you will go?"

"Vicki wants to go up north to Dulce, in the New Mexico Territory, where she grew up."

Frank shook hands with Cade. "Thank you, Cade. You be careful getting out of here. Evans is out there somewhere."

Cade let out a loud laugh. "Let that little runt come to me. We'll have a good old-fashioned knife fight." Vicki, Cade saw, was giving him a displeased look, with Cade not staying on task. "Nice to work with you, fellas. If you're ever up North, stop by and say hello." Then Cade scurried off to finish loading his wagons.

Cade and Vicki weren't the only ones in a hurry. The Cowboys were behind Evans and had to make up for lost time to catch him. They quickly finished loading their supplies and rode off. Ben was a good resource since this was Apache land, and with his help, they could make great strides in catching up with Evans, who was presumed to be heading to his hideout up in the mountains. The beautiful trees and the countryside impressed the Cowboys. This terrain was what Frank, John, and Boyd had hoped they would find in the New Mexico Territory. They were looking for a place to settle down outside Texas and loved the scenery in the New Mexico Territory. Ben was just happy to be on Apache land. It displeased him that a criminal like Evans was using Apache land to hide. It was his duty, he felt, to track down this killer and bring him to justice.

Eventually, he tracked Evans to his hideout, which was an old cabin up on a hillside, surrounded by trees. This would help the Cowboys hide within the tree covering. They slowly spread out and surrounded the cabin, waiting for Evans to come out.

It was a chilly morning marked by light fog, providing even more cover for the Cowboys.

As the Cowboys waited in the darkness for Tunstall's killer, they saw a large raccoon scurry out of the bushes near the cabin. Not too far behind the large raccoon came two medium-sized raccoons. They were doing their scouting around the cabin, hoping to find food left out by the occupants. While the big raccoon was searching for food, his traveling partners began wrestling instead of searching for their meal for the night. Suddenly, the large raccoon stood up on its back feet, and with its front paws, extended wide, which resembled a gunfighter getting ready to draw his guns. Boyd, who was closer to the raccoons, quietly laughed at the performance by the furry creatures. The two smaller raccoons, seemingly knowing their larger traveling companion was not happy, stopped wrestling and resumed their food search. Once a few minutes passed and the raccoons realized there was nothing for them, they scurried off behind the cabin and disappeared.

As the Cowboys returned their focus to the cabin, they began to hear sounds like someone was walking inside the cabin. This was highlighted by the wood flooring that cabins had in the area. The Cowboys raised their guns toward the cabin door in preparation for Evans to appear. They all heard the door to the cabin creak open, with no movement at first, then they could make out a head peeking outside of the cabin door. After a few moments, the rest of the door opened completely.

Evans came out the front door and walked to the end of the porch. His bald head and long, bushy beard were easily recognizable. He started urinating off the edge of the porch, oblivious to the Cowboys quietly watching him. He was armed with a Henry rifle, but he made the mistake of setting it down on the porch railing.

Ben, closest to the porch, quickly made his move. The fastest of the Cowboys, he sprinted across the porch toward Evans. Before Evans knew what happened, Ben had tackled him, and they both flew off the edge of the porch into the brush. Evans attempted to put up a struggle at first; however, he was soon subdued by Ben, who had quickly placed his knife on the throat of the bandit. The other three Cowboys rushed to the scene, only to see Ben safely sitting on top of Evans, who was crying, begging the Apache to not kill him. The Cowboys had agreed to take him to Justice of the Peace Jay Wilson alive, if possible. Jesse Evans' fate would be up to the court to decide.

Evans' capture firmly established the Cowboys as trusted enforcers in the New Mexico Territory. However, they felt that their time in Lincoln County was coming to an end. This was because some of the other Regulators, led by Billy the Kid, were causing havoc in the area. The Cowboys, not wanting to be associated with them, left the Lincoln County Regulators to go on their own. They agreed to head up North to the Chama area, which was near Dulce, where Cade was moving to. Ben advised the Cowboys to reach out to Navajo Chief Lonewolf for safe passage through the Navajo territory.

The Cowboys wanted a fresh start, something better.

"If we are going up North for a fresh start," Frank said, "how about we start our own Regulators group?"

"I agree," John replied. "We've always talked about being a force that fights for people who can't fight for themselves. Starting our Regulators group is exactly what we need to do."

"If we are to do this," Ben said, "it can't be associated with any lawmen group, to avoid rancher influence."

"I agree, but if we are not Regulators," Boyd replied, "then what do we call ourselves?"

There was a brief pause.

"We will call ourselves American Cowboys," John said. "That will set us apart from the others because we will offer protection to those who cannot protect themselves."

They all looked at each other and nodded in agreement.

"American Cowboys because we represent what America is," Frank said. "We have different backgrounds, but we strive for the same thing."

"What are we striving for, Frank?" Boyd asked.

"Freedom," Frank replied. "Freedom for people to live their lives without fear of it being taken away because they cannot protect themselves."

The Cowboys looked at each other and smiled.

"We are the American Cowboys," John said.

The Cowboys said their goodbyes to one another and agreed to meet up North after they had departed Lincoln County. John went to get Jane, and Frank accompanied him to get Michael.

The Cowboys rode off to their destinations, more determined than ever for their future. Their future was as the American Cowboys.

Thirteen

The Shooter

1882

Oscar could tell by the soaring ponderosa pine trees that he was not in Texas anymore.

Seeking adventure and new life experiences had driven him to leave Texas. The further he went, the more he knew this was the right decision, especially with his travels taking him through the New Mexico Territory. The desert setting, with what appeared to be painted mountains, was mesmerizing. Brown, red, and tan colors covered everything on the horizon. The stories he had read about the New Mexico Territory in his youth in Texas all seemed to be true. The wide-open spaces with unique scenery offered travelers what seemed to be endless options to roam. His family had wanted him to stay home and help manage their South Texas ranch with his brother, Ryan. This option did not appeal to his adventurous spirit, though. Oscar wanted to experience the West, which spoke of cowboys and Indians. This was the life he sought. This was why he chose the life of a wandering cowboy instead of a tied-down rancher.

His wandering had led him to Dulce, which was a stop on his way to Colorado. A stop at this village would be welcomed by this tired cowboy. Even though he was a young man, at seventeen years old, the long days riding a horse were exhausting. The rough terrain and hot temperatures were a force to be reckoned with. Oscar was five foot seven inches tall, with light brown skin and black hair. His eyes were brown and gave birth to his brother, Ryan, calling him Marrones. He was glad no one in the New Mexico Territory knew that nickname since he was not in favor of it. The thought of it made him think of his brother and the family he'd left behind in Texas. Loneliness and missing them had made his travels harder. Once he explored Colorado, he would return to Texas unless he found something to be a part of in this territory.

Upon riding into Dulce, he was immediately enchanted. The backdrop to the village was a booming mountain range. Tall pines surrounded the area and went on for as far as one could see. The village was bustling with wagons carrying pioneers. Dulce was an Apache trading village where locals and travelers could get supplies, The travelers were usually pioneers heading off for their journey into a new world westward. A world that could be cruel to new-comers and which would be the demise of many. Oscar stopped at the first saloon he came to. Dismounting his horse, he tied her up and headed inside.

"Barkeep, give me a whiskey and make it a double," Oscar said once he made it to the bar of the saloon. He had wanted whiskey for the last couple of days since he had drunk all of his.

"How's the poker in this place?" he said to the barkeep.

"The game is good if you can play. The big game, though, is tomorrow at the range."

Intrigued, Oscar enquired, "What type of game is at the range?"

"Shooting contest son. We have one every month. Big money to win if you can shoot."

Oscar was interested in the contest. He was an excellent shot and had won plenty of shooting contests. Through experience, he knew to keep his interest down. An eager player in these games for money would run off lesser players trying to win. That meant the winning prize may go down. "Thank you, barkeep. I'll keep my options open," Oscar said as he turned around and leaned his back against the bar.

"I'd be careful kid, that contest is not for young ones," Boyd said while walking up to the bar to order a drink. "Give me a beer, Pete." He knew the bartender well since moving into the area.

Oscar, perturbed by the stranger's comment yet never taking his eyes off his stare into the saloon, calmly said, "In my experience, old is slow, so I reckon it will be okay." Then he turned and looked at Boyd.

Boyd, with a slight grin on his face, knowing his comment had triggered the young cowboy, quickly retorted, "Easy kid, don't let the old fool you. They may take a little longer to get there, but they don't miss."

The two cowboys stared at each other briefly, Boyd smiling and Oscar not breaking his look. "Alright Boyd, leave the kid alone and go get us a card game started," John said to the cowboys while walking up to the bar. Boyd patted Oscar on the shoulder, then slowly left the bar to do as John had asked.

"Don't take it personally, kid. Boyd likes to give young guys a hard time to get in their head before a game is coming up." Oscar nodded his head at John, then looked back at the card games going on in the saloon. "My name is John Rose. What brings you up to these parts?"

"Oscar Martinez is the name. I'm traveling up from Texas looking for adventure."

"Adventure, you say," John replied. "You didn't have to leave Texas for that. It's full of possibilities." John turned to Pete and took a glass of water that was already prepared for him. "Thank you, Pete. What do I owe you for the guys?"

"There's never a charge for the American Cowboys. That's the least I could do for you after all you've done around here."

"We appreciate that, but it is unnecessary," John replied. We're happy to help when needed."

Pete nodded his head, then said, "No one else could have done what you Cowboys did. You are always welcome here."

This piqued Oscar's interest. He had heard stories of the American Cowboys and how they had rescued kidnapped people and brought bandits to justice. The stories that stood out the most were about the train rescues. Stories like these had driven him to this area, and now he was next to the legend.

Looking toward John, he said, "American Cowboys, you ride with them?"

"Yes, I ride with the Cowboys." John paused before adding, "I see you've heard of us."

Oscar was now fully engaged with John and said, "Of course, the American Cowboys are all the talk in the New Mexico Territory." This caused John to grin. He was sure Lincoln County was not too fond of him or his friends. "How did you help the bartender?"

"They saved my wife from bandits, kid. They have saved many people," Pete said from behind the bar. "We are grateful for what they do."

Despite Oscar's impression, John opted for a less public approach. They had not started the Cowboys to be recognized for doing good. They just wanted to help those who could not help themselves.

"Oscar, the real reward is helping people. The recognition is never a consideration."

Frank, just entering the saloon, walked up to the bar and said, "John, let's go have a seat. We just had a letter come in from Durango requesting some help." Frank paused after looking at the young man speaking with John and said, "How are you, cowboy? Name is Frank Morgan."

"Pleasure to meet you, Frank. I'm Oscar from Texas." The size of the cowboy he had also read about surprised Oscar. Never did he think a cowboy could be so big.

Frank nodded his head at the young cowboy in acknowledgment then went to join Boyd, who had found a table.

John picked up his glass of water and turned to go join Frank. He then stopped, turned to Oscar, and said, "Why don't you join us? We can talk about that shooting contest for tomorrow."

Oscar did not have to think long about the offer and followed John to their table.

The Cowboys played each other in a card game. They enjoyed one another's company and Oscar was a good fit for the group. During the game, Ben entered the saloon and joined the group. After a short time, Ben, Frank, and Boyd left the table to move the horses to the back of the saloon, which was the custom in the evening. Boyd patted Oscar on the shoulder as he passed behind him and grinned. He had continued to give the young cowboy a hard time during the card game. Oscar had joked back with Boyd, and they quickly became comfortable around each other. All the American Cowboys felt like Oscar was a good fit for the group, but only time would tell.

"So, Oscar, did we talk you into the game tomorrow?"

After a brief pause, he looked at John and said, "Yes, I will shoot tomorrow. I ask one thing."

Puzzled, John replied, "What request do you have, son?"

"I would like to join the Cowboys. Let me prove tomorrow that I'm a good enough shot to be an American Cowboy."

John looked at Oscar momentarily, then said, "Being an American Cowboy has more to do than being an excellent shot. Shooting is sometimes the easiest part."

John knew the most important character a cowboy had to have was knowing why you are shooting. It would be a while before they knew if Oscar would be a good fit for the American Cowboys. But the potential of the young cowboy intrigued John.

"Let's see how you do tomorrow, then we will talk."

Oscar nodded in agreement, then the men finished their drinks while talking about Texas.

The shooting contest brought out the best shooters in the northern New Mexico Territory. There were thirty-two shooters in the contest, including Boyd and Oscar. It helped that there was a five-dollar prize for the victor. After great shots by the two cowboys, they were soon in the finals against each other. A coin toss decided that Boyd would shoot first. Boyd was a dead eye and could hit a flying crow at a respectful distance. He lined up his shots and hit the center mark on four of his five targets. The fifth shot was only half an inch away from the center. Oscar would have to be perfect to win. He was determined to come away with the win so he might gain the American Cowboys' favor and be invited to join their group. The Cowboys were exactly what he was hoping to find before going back to Texas. This group was for him and could be the reason to stay in this area.

"Don't miss, kid. There's no prize for second," Boyd said while leaving the shooter's table.

Oscar smiled, then replied, "There are two prizes for being old—grey hair and poor eyesight." Boyd laughed at this response and went to sit with Frank, John, and Ben.

Oscar lined up his shots, exhaled deeply, and then systematically hit all five targets dead center line. He had won the tournament.

While Oscar was collecting his prize money, the four American Cowboys looked at one another and nodded in agreement. They would let Oscar ride with their group temporarily. He had proven his skills with his gun; now he would have to do the same with his character.

The American Cowboys were growing in reputation. Now they may be growing in size as well.

Fourteen

The Kidnap

1890

Nizhoni enjoyed being an early riser. She loved seeing the sunrise on the horizon and slowly lighting up the landscape. Walking barefoot in the wet grass and listening to the birds sing helped her feel renewed. Her father told her that she taught the importance of Navajo land to their people. She took pride in that statement and made a point of teaching others about the beauty of Navajo lands. These mornings would make her think of Two-Rivers. They had become close and she knew they might be together when the time was right. These thoughts made her happy, but also nervous. Life was moving fast for this young Navajo, and she needed time to think about these big potential changes.

On this morning, Nizhoni was out gathering crops with twelve other women from her tribe. Following the Navajo tradition, she had started gathering when she was a young girl. She wanted to make sure she did her part for the betterment of the tribe The women worked systematically as a team to collect the crops. Doing this brought her much happiness and a sense of fulfillment. These crops fed the entire tribe and the gathering of it nourished a strong sense of community among the women.

This, Dane knew, was the perfect time and place to kidnap Nizhoni. His scouts had been watching the Navajo and studying their patterns to gauge when to act. They found that when the women went to gather food, the Navajo warriors did not accompany them and went to hunt instead—it was the only time the women were left alone. Dane knew that the rest of the tribe would not know what had happened until after they kidnapped Nizhoni. It would take even longer for the warriors to return from hunting and mount a search for the Chief's daughter. The timing and place were perfect.

Dane and his men watched the women come to the fields and start working. There were, just as his scouts had found out, no Navajo warriors with them for protection. The women, who were busy gathering, did not notice the rustling in the bushes as the men approached them. Dane and ten gunmen crept through the fields. Evil was among the Navajo women, and they did not realize it.

Dane and his men attacked Nizhoni and the other Navajo women with a viciousness usually reserved for wartime. Dane grabbed one Navajo woman at the front and sliced her neck with his knife. Before the others knew what was happening, the gunmen had already begun attacking them. Dane made his way to the beautiful young Nizhoni, who, witnessing the brutal murder of her friends, was in shock and could not move. One of the older women grabbed her and said, "Run, Nizhoni! Run to the village for help!"

Nizhoni snapped out of her frozen state and ran as fast as she could. Behind her, Dane sunk his Bowie knife deep into the back of the older woman. She fell to the ground, dead. Dane whistled for his horse, which caught up to him, and he mounted it in full stride. Dane, part of the mounted division during the Civil War, was an expert rider, so it was only a matter of time before he was close to

Nizhoni. Noticing this, a Navajo woman tried to swing a large stick at him, but Dane pulled out his scattergun and shot her.

When Dane caught up to Nizhoni, he cut her off with his horse. She screamed. He aimed his gun at her and put a finger to his mouth, making a shushing sound.

"Hello, Nizhoni. Let's go for a ride." He then yelled out to his men, "Leave one alive to send our message. Kill the rest."

Once Dane's men finished killing the Navajo women, he forced Nizhoni onto his horse.

As ordered, one Navajo woman was left alive to take a message back to Chief Lonewolf informing him of the kidnap of his daughter and the Baron's demands. The demands were direct: the Navajo tribe was to sell their lands to the Baron and not cause any disturbance to the railroad construction. If the Navajo refused, Nizhoni would be sent back in pieces; if the Navajo agreed, then they were to meet the Baron in Silverton to sign an agreement.

The frightened Navajo woman took the message and turned to walk away. She was terrified, fearing that any moment would bring her death at the hands of the evil bandits.

Watching her friend walk off into the distance, Nizhoni wept. She didn't know whether she would ever see her people or Two-Rivers again.

Watching the Navajo woman leave the bloody field with his message, Dane smiled. The plan was in motion.

Fifteen

A Plea

Sorrow followed Chief Lonewolf, Two-Rivers, and the other Navajo riders on this journey to Chama. The news that the Baron's men had kidnapped his daughter crushed Chief Lonewolf's spirit. Everything in his body told him to assemble a war party to go rescue his daughter. However, experience and council told him it would only lead to new battles with the US Cavalry, losing more Navajo land and, probably, the death of his daughter. Two-Rivers wanted revenge and attempted to form a war party, but Chief Lonewolf intervened and advised patience for the young warrior. He knew Two-Rivers cared for his daughter, but the Navajo people must come first.

Years ago, Chief Lonewolf had met a man, John Rose, and helped him and his men move from Lincoln County to Chama. John and his companions, including an Apache, were fleeing the Lincoln County War. They called themselves the American Cowboys and promised to take care of the land if Chief Lonewolf gave them safe passage. His only hope of avoiding a costly war with the Baron and saving his daughter was to ask the American Cowboys for help. They had become legendary since their first meeting and had lived up to their promise to protect the lands. As Chief Lonewolf approached John's home with a plea for help, his heart grew heavier with every step his horse took.

Jane was hanging laundry on the clothesline outside their ranch house. John had built the ranch house from the pine trees on their land. The house was large enough for them to raise the family they were planning. Jane insisted he build a large porch so they could sit and enjoy the beautiful scenery that surrounded the cabin. The beautiful ponderosa pine trees that soared to the skyline and the nearby rolling mountains were everything she had dreamed about, her forever home. Some trees grew as tall as eighty feet and produced large pinecones that lay at their bases after falling from the branches they used to reside upon. The rolling hills surrounding the property peeked just above the tree line as if the land was watching what they did beyond the trees. In the distance, she saw the Indians approaching. She knew John was friendly with the Navajo, but she was uncertain about the other tribes in the area.

John was in their cabin when Jane burst inside to tell him. Grabbing his Colt Peacemaker, he ran outside. Though he had a good relationship with the nearby tribes, it was difficult to know if the visitors were coming for peaceful reasons. John quickly noticed that it was a Navajo tribe, being led by Chief Lonewolf.

"Let's get ready to receive our friends," John said.

There appeared to be about ten men riding with Chief Lonewolf, and the Roses would be friendly hosts.

Chief Lonewolf passed through the gate of the ranch and greeted the couple.

"Hello, Chief. To what do we owe the pleasure of this visit?" John asked.

"We have a problem I need to discuss with you and your wife. May we go inside?"

"Of course," Jane said, "Please come in."

John, Jane, and Chief Lonewolf made their way into the cabin, while Two-Rivers and the rest of the riding party tended to their horses.

Something was wrong with Chief Lonewolf, John could tell. He wasn't his normal self and had a look of grief on his face.

Chief Lonewolf did not waste time. He immediately told John and Jane what had happened to his daughter outside their village. Chief Lonewolf told them that if the Navajo attempted to rescue Nizhoni, he feared the US Cavalry would intervene. He looked into John's eyes and said, "You asked me for help once, and we helped you. I'm asking for your help now in getting my daughter back from these men."

Hearing Chief Lonewolf's plea, Jane grew anxious. She knew the dangers her husband faced every time he went on a rescue attempt. But she also understood that the Navajo Chief coming to her husband meant this was his only option. And this was going to be dangerous. The entire territory knew that the Baron's main gunman was Dane—the man who had killed Michael, and now the man the American Cowboys must confront to rescue Nizhoni. John knew this as well.

"I'm sorry for everything that happened to your daughter and the other women," Jane said. "What will the US Cavalry do if the Navajo get involved?"

"The Navajo will lose," Chief Lonewolf said. "They will make more reservations for my people."

"That is probably the Baron's plan. He just wants your tribe out of the way," John said. "Where are they holding her?"

"Our scouts have learned that they are holding her in Alamosa but will soon move her to Silverton." Chief Lonewolf replied.

"Is there any other way to save your daughter? This will be a dangerous mission for my husband." Jane asked.

The Chief looked at Jane. "This is the only way for me to get my daughter back alive and save our lands."

The right thing to do, John knew, was to rescue Nizhoni. He looked at Jane.

She nodded her head. This, she realized, was going to be her husband's most dangerous mission. But it had to be done. The Navajo had suffered enough, and no father should have his child taken from him. She had already witnessed this with the death of Michael, and she didn't want to see another father lose his child at the hands of Dane.

"As God is my witness, I will get your daughter back from these evil men and return her to you," John said. "Their run of terror in this territory is about to end."

Chief Lonewolf expressed his thanks. "The Navajo people will help you find information about their travel plans. But to ensure the tribe's safety, they cannot join the rescue. I will send three riders to meet the Navajo scouts from Alamosa, including Two-Rivers, who will receive the information about the Baron's travel situation. They will then meet you near Durango and give you the information. We will never forget your generosity and sacrifice."

"Thank you, Chief. I need you to do one thing for me." John said.

"Of course. What do you need of me?"

"Send a message to the Baron that you will meet him in Silverton," John replied.

Puzzled, the Chief asked, "Why would we do that?"

"We want the Baron thinking the Navajo will come to Silverton, so he will have most of his gunmen there."

"How will that help you?" Jane asks.

"Fewer gunmen will be protecting Nizhoni, making her rescue easier."

This made good sense to the Chief. "When will you attempt to rescue her?"

"I don't know right now, but we will not have long before she is moved to Silverton," John replied.

The Chief agreed and thanked the Roses for their hospitality.

He then left the cabin, walked over to his horse, and mounted it. The other Navajo mounted their horses and rode them to their Chief. Two-Rivers spoke with him briefly and then looked at John and nodded. He then rode off with two other Navajo riders who were going to accompany him to meet the Navajo scouts from Alamosa. John and Jane stood on the porch and watched the Navajo ride off one by one. Chief Lonewolf stopped and waved, his face covered with worry before he disappeared into the distance.

Jane looked at John. "You're going to need Frank."

Sixteen

The Cowboys' Last Ride

John knew that his visit to Frank would be difficult.

After losing his wife, the only things that comforted him were his faith and Michael. John was not a parent yet; he didn't know the full depth of sorrow Frank was going through. But he knew what it would mean to lose Jane. Losing your wife had to be one of the hardest things a man can go through. Even worse, he imagined, must be losing a child.

Throughout the years, John had grown close to Frank, and he knew how special his relationship with his wife had been. He remembered the late nights they had spent around the campfire, telling old war stories, and discussing the Bible—moments John knew he would cherish forever. He remembered the first time he had met Maybelle, a beautiful woman with a great laugh. She had always asked him to take care of Frank, a request he took seriously to this day.

And now, he was going to invite Frank to join a dangerous rescue mission. The only thing that might convince Frank, John knew, was the opportunity to confront Dane.

John made his way to Frank's cabin in Brazos. Since Michael's death, he spent his time in solitude in his cabin. It was where Frank and Michael had moved to after leaving Lincoln County. The family Frank had dreamed of having was now gone, and he was left alone. His faith had always carried him, but now he felt lost. To take his own life, he knew, was wrong, and he refused to die before avenging Michael's death. He had told this to John during his last visit.

John approached the cabin, taking in its look of desolation and emptiness. Frank had always kept it nice, but he had obviously stopped caring for it after Michael's death. He rode up to the front porch and dismounted. He walked to the front door of the cabin and noticed it swinging open.

"Frank, it's John. I'm here to check on you."

No one answered. John drew his Peacemaker, prepared for anything. It was common for bandits to invade someone's home with bad intentions in mind. If that was the case, he needed to be prepared.

"I'm back here," Frank said solemnly from inside the cabin.

John holstered his gun and went inside. The cabin was dim, with light only coming through the windows. He noticed Frank's Colt Peacemaker and gun belt lying on the floor. Then he noticed him sitting on the floor.

"How are you doing, Frank?"

He looked up at John and then looked away. Frank looked terrible; he looked broken.

"Navajo Chief Lonewolf wants the Cowboys to ride for him. They have kidnapped his daughter. The Navajo cannot attempt to get her back without risking the US Cavalry getting involved."

Frank sat motionless, staring at Michael's cowboy hat, which he was holding in his hands.

"The Cowboys are her only hope. I need your help, or she will die." John then quoted Philippians 2:4: *Let each of you look not only to his interests but also to the interests of others.* "Join me on this mission, brother. We are her only hope."

Frank did not understand why John did not just let him be. He did not care about anything anymore. He just wanted to be left alone. He did not appreciate John quoting the scripture either. He remembered that John did not have a relationship with God until he met him. The meaning of his being was gone with the death of his son.

"No, I will not help you. The American Cowboys are done," he said, without taking his eyes off Michael's cowboy hat. "Now go away and let me be. And save the scriptures for someone else."

John knew he had one ace in his pocket. "I do not know your pain, and I pray I never do. You have suffered more loss than two men combined. Now, you have the chance to stop another father from suffering this grief. You can stay here and wait for death to find you, or you can get up and help the American Cowboys save her."

John paused for a moment.

Frank did not budge and kept his eyes on Michael's hat.

John turned and walked to the door before stopping in the doorway. "If it makes any difference, it was Dane who kidnapped his daughter. He is the one we will go after."

Frank was shocked. Ever since the botched El Paso rescue, he had only thought about avenging his son's death. By going on this mission with the American Cowboys, the vengeance he was so desperately seeking could be his. And John was right—he did not want another father to experience what he was experiencing. Rescuing the girl and returning her to her father would be a worthy cause for the American Cowboys. But more than anything, he was desperate to avenge his son's death by killing Dane.

He looked up from Michael's cowboy hat. "I'm in."

John nodded his head. "Let's ride and go round up the American Cowboys."

***

Boyd, Ben, and Oscar were hired to work at the Log Cabin Ranch. John could have ridden there first, but he knew Frank had to say yes first. If he did, then the others would be in.

But there was one issue remaining: this would be the first time Boyd and Frank were going to see each other since Michael's death—a fact that was not forgotten by Frank and John as they rode toward the ranch.

Getting back on his horse helped Frank. His thoughts were about Michael and the chance to avenge his death. His hatred for Dane now had an outlet. He remembered when Michael was born, how proud he was to be his father, and the times they played together around the house with his wife. Michael had made his life complete, and now he was gone because of Dane. Frank then thought of Boyd, and how his inaction had led to his son's death. He felt betrayed. Frank didn't know how he would feel when he saw Boyd.

"I know you have issues with Boyd. I need you to be peaceful," John said.

This statement did not please Frank. He looked at John, then turned his head back to their path. "We will discuss El Paso; I promise you that."

"I understand, but we have to focus on rescuing Nizhoni first. We cannot do that if you and Boyd kill each other."

Frank paused before saying, "He should not have laid his gun down on that train. That decision took my son from me."

Both of them rode in silence for a while after that statement. John had no answers to this dilemma. He felt Boyd had no other choice than to put his rifle down. But Frank would not want to hear that.

"He owes me an answer as to why that was a good idea. Michael died anyway. Just take the shot and give my boy a chance to live."

"I know you two need to talk. Promise me you will wait until after this mission is completed."

Frank thought about this request. Deep down, he knew John was right to wait. Frank knew he had no choice but to honor John's request. "I promise I will not confront him until after the rescue— this will be a hard promise to keep."

"Thank you. Your son meant a lot to me and Jane. We miss him every day."

All John could think of was Jane being pregnant. All his life he had wanted a child, and now his wish was going to be fulfilled. He longed to be a good father. His father had been terrible, and he vowed not to put his children through what he went through. He was thankful for Jane and couldn't believe how well his family was doing. But he also felt sad for Frank. He had lost everything, and John was now gaining everything his friend had lost. John had not told Frank about Jane's pregnancy; he didn't know how to. He had planned to reveal it to him before the El Paso rescue, but then he waited until they completed the job. Now he had to wait even longer.

At the Log Cabin Ranch, Boyd, Ben, and Oscar had stable work; it wasn't the best, but the pay was good. They were working on a fencing project that covered the ranch's southern portion. The air was cool and breezy, which was normal for fall in the New Mexico Territory. After this, they would direct the cattle on the ranch to the new fenced area they had built. They weren't keen on building barbed wire fencing where they once freely rode across the prairies, but they needed the money and didn't have any other choice. Of the three, Ben was the most restless. He informed Boyd and Oscar that he would leave after they moved the cattle. He roamed free and didn't consider ranching jobs much different from life on a reservation. Boyd and Oscar understood, but they were sad to witness the American Cowboys continuing to separate.

While Ben inspected the fencing, he noticed riders approaching in the distance. He alerted the others, who quickly grabbed their rifles. They knew one had to always be prepared for the worst when riders approached. The riders drew closer, and they saw it was Frank and John. Boyd froze and grew anxious. Deep down, he thought Frank was coming to kill him. As he and John approached, Boyd tightened his grip on his rifle.

The tension in the air was thick. Frank's eyes never left Boyd's, who was still holding onto his Winchester rifle. This was the reunion Boyd was dreading. He knew Frank blamed him for Michael's death. Boyd just did not want to harm Michael with a careless shot. Also, he didn't think Dane would kill him. That was then, and this was now.

After a few tense moments, John hopped off his horse.

"Gentlemen, what happened in the past between us will have to wait for a resolution. Navajo Chief Lonewolf's daughter, Nizhoni, is in the custody of Dane and the Baron, and the American Cowboys need to rescue her. If we don't intervene and save Nizhoni, she will surely die."

The Cowboys looked at each other to gauge their reactions.

John continued, "The Navajo cannot attempt to save her because the US Cavalry would get involved. They won't survive another Long Walk. They need our help. I'm asking you all to join me for one last ride, so that we may save Nizhoni and bring Dane to justice."

John looked at each of the Cowboys and gave them a minute to think about it. "What do you say, fellas? Will you ride with the American Cowboys once again?"

The Cowboys looked at each other, and one by one, agreed. He thanked them.

"One thing before we go," Frank said. "Dane is mine to kill. Understand?"

Everyone nodded in agreement, minus Oscar. If he had the chance to take Dane out, he would take it. Frank did not notice this from Oscar; his eyes were still fixed on Boyd's. After a moment, Frank nodded to Boyd, and he nodded back. They both knew they had this job to take care of, which outweighed what had happened between them.

John broke the silence. "Let's go to the bunkhouse and get your gear ready."

Seventeen

Last Night Home

John was friendly with the Log Cabin Ranch owner, Gaylon Townsend. He explained to him what was happening with the Navajo and the Baron. He was sympathetic, as his wife Zelda was part Cherokee, and he agreed to assist them in any way he could. Boyd and Oscar agreed to return to the ranch after the rescue mission was complete.

They loaded their gear and headed to John's home for the night to rest and plan the rescue. The scenery in the Northern New Mexico Territory was breathtaking. The beauty of the rolling landscape, littered with soaring ponderosa pine trees and high mountain peaks, was perfect. Occasionally deer would sprint across the grass, almost daring the Cowboys for a hunt. The peacefulness offered on this ride was a nice relief for the Cowboys, who were headed for a difficult mission. Chama was located outside the Apache reservation in the Rocky Mountains. John and Jane loved this area so much that they had built their home there. This land was what the Cowboys had dreamed about when they thought about where they wanted to live after leaving Lincoln County. John was happy that the American Cowboys were back together, but his thoughts kept going back to Jane.

Jane was preparing dinner for the Cowboys. She knew that all of them, out of the love they had for each other, would say yes to John's request to ride one more time as the American Cowboys. She knew it was the right thing for them to do. But she was concerned about John's safety. The last time they left for a rescue, Michael never returned. She knew how dangerous these rescues were, and it was going to be even more dangerous this time—apart from being good, they had to be lucky to pull off this rescue. Then she realized that she needed to have faith in them and pray for their safety.

She heard John and Frank outside. She went to the door and, seeing all the American Cowboys back together, smiled. But there was no greater joy for her than having John back home.

John and Frank were the first to reach the cabin. Jane ran up to John and wrapped her arms around him. Frank immediately noticed that Jane was showing. He was surprised.

"Hello, honey. I missed you," John said.

"I'm so happy to see you," Jane replied. Then they kissed for a moment until Frank cleared his throat.

"Nice to see you too, Jane. It's been a while," Frank said.

Jane hugged him. "It's been too long, and I'm so sorry about Michael."

Frank looked at her for a moment. "I appreciate your kind words and the food you sent. It was mighty kind."

Jane nodded at Frank but was struck by his eyes. They always looked joyful, but today, there was sorrow in them. "Just know we are here for you if you need anything."

"Thank you. And congratulations. I see you are expecting."

"Thank you. We didn't want to tell you until you were ready."

"We know you are hurting and didn't want to make matters worse," John said.

It was then he realized that they had not told him because he was grieving for Michael. He appreciated that they were looking out for him, that they were respecting Michael's memory. But it also made him sorrowful; it made him wish he could turn back time to when Maybelle and Michael were still alive.

"I appreciate you both. Did you want the guys to set up camp in the bunkhouse?" Frank said, trying to change the subject. He didn't want any of them to get in the way of the couple's privacy.

"That will be fine," Jane said. "Tell the guys to come and fix their plates. Dinner is ready."

He nodded and went to give the Cowboys the message. The Cowboys were happy that Jane had made them dinner, and they thanked her for her kindness. In their rush to head to Chama, they had not eaten. They filled their plates with food and headed outside to sit by the campfire and take in some fresh mountain air. They also wanted to give John and Jane some time together; this would be their last night together for a few days.

Now alone in the cabin, John and Jane discussed plans for the ranch, as if nothing else was happening. Their talk soon turned to children and their future. He had been elated ever since Jane had told him they were expecting. He had dreamed of little ones running around the cabin and the ranch. The memories they would create filled him with joy.

"So, how is our little boy doing?" John asked, rubbing Jane's pregnant stomach.

"Oh, she is growing and kicking every day. Mainly kicking."

They laughed. "This little blessing from God is just ready to come on out and join us," John said.

"Well, not soon enough, because momma's back is hurting."

"Oh Jane, I'm sorry. Let's go sit in the living room so you can rest."

They went into the living room, sat by the fireplace, and spent most of the night discussing what the future had in store for them. They intentionally did not mention the upcoming rescue. Some things were better left unsaid.

Frank and the rest of the cowboys gathered around the fire and began discussing the rescue. He and John had made some plans while they were on their way to the Log Cabin Ranch. Their plan would only work if they worked together and pushed their horses harder than ever before. The window for the rescue was tight—they had to be perfect. If not, Nizhoni might die, and the American Cowboys might not make it back home.

Eighteen

Ride to Colorado

Saying goodbye to Jane was never easy for John.

He walked over to her and wrapped his arms around her. His firm embrace was all she needed to say goodbye. She felt comfort and love in his arms. Released from his embrace, she looked into his eyes.

"I love you. You take care of yourself."

She watched him walk away to his horse and mount it.

He turned to her and said, "Love you, Jane," then rode toward the ranch gates, where the Cowboys were waiting.

They were about to start their ride to Colorado. First, they would head to Dulce to meet Cade for supplies.

"Did you say your goodbyes?" Frank asked.

"Yes, sir. We're ready to ride."

Frank let out a rare slight grin, the thought of vengeance on his mind, and yelled, "American Cowboys, pull out!"

From the porch, Jane watched the Cowboys ride away. She didn't feel the tears until they ran down her cheeks. "Come back to us, John. We need you," she said, caressing her stomach.

On their way to Dulce, the Cowboys witnessed the beautiful landscape of the Northern New Mexico Territory. The trees that seemed never-ending, the running spring water, the singing birds— all of it helped them relax. A large buck emerged from the forest to investigate the noise, as if to let them know that they were passing through his territory. The air was crisp and smelled of pine. It reminded the Cowboys of Lincoln County, but this was more grandiose.

Dulce was right on the continental divide, which the Cowboys noticed because of the thin air since the elevation was just under 6,700 ft. Dulce was a beautiful area and a favorite of the Cowboys to visit. Here, the Cowboys would get their supplies. They had to be in Durango when the Baron's train arrived. They weren't sure when his train would pass through Durango. They were hopeful, that Navajo scouts would give them that information. They needed a day and a half to get there by horseback. The terrain would be rough, so they needed to make the most of their time. Under different circumstances, they would have visited Pete's Saloon, but time would not permit that.

When they reached Dulce, they headed for the trading post. Their old friends Cade and Vicki from Lincoln County owned the trading post. Cade had acquired this valuable trading post on Apache territory because of Vicki's Apache heritage. A black woman named Teresa worked for Cade and was friends with Jane, and John had planned to ask Cade whether Teresa could go to Chama and help Jane.

"Well, I'll be a cross-eyed donkey, the American Cowboys ride again, and they're in my trading post," Cade said. He then let out his boisterous laugh. "As I live and breathe, how the heck are you guys?"

"We're well, old friend. How's the trading business?" Frank asked.

"It's great. Rolling in money and loving life." The rest of the Cowboys exchanged pleasantries with Cade. Then they split up and started gathering the supplies.

Cade walked over to Frank. "I'm so sorry about Michael. The worst thing that could happen to a man."

"Thank you, Cade. What do you know about how the Baron travels by train? Like, how many guns travel with him?"

Cade rubbed his head while he thought. Cade knew most things about everyone, and Frank knew he probably had some good information they could use.

"He travels with at least ten guns, maybe more, depending on what he's dealing with. They strategically position the gunmen throughout the train. Some will be with him in his train car for protection. If he thinks you Cowboys are coming, there may be more gunmen on the train. Best keep it as quiet as you can."

John walked up behind Frank and Cade. "Is it still quiet that we're coming?"

Cade let out another loud laugh. "The only people who know you're coming will not tell that scoundrel. Look, we go back a long way, and we're friends, but this is going to be difficult. Have your head on a swivel and shoot to kill."

"Thank you, Cade," John said. "I have a favor to ask."

"Anything for an old Regulator."

"Can you send Teresa to my place in Chama to help Jane while I'm gone?"

"Absolutely. But it'll cost you." Cade laughed again. "Vicki can help me out around here until you get home."

After they were done, the cowboys thanked Cade for his hospitality and walked out of the trading post to load their supplies.

"You ready for this?" John asked Frank.

"I've been ready since El Paso."

***

After a hard day's ride, the Cowboys stopped to rest the horses and camped outside of Durango. They were preparing food when the Navajos emerged from the tree line, practically unnoticed. Ben was the first to spot them approaching the campground on their horses, and he alerted the others, who grabbed their guns. John recognized Two-Rivers and informed the other Cowboys that the Navajo were friendly. The Cowboys welcomed them into the camp. After dismounting their horses, they all sat around the campfire to discuss what the Navajo riders had learned from the Alamosa scouts. John hoped they had information on when to expect the train at Durango.

The scouts had found that the sides of the Baron's train would be vulnerable. His gunmen would be spread throughout the train cars and focus on the front and rear of the train. The terrain they passed through provided cover in the form of trees and mountain cliffs to the sides. Also, the Baron had bought the story that the Navajo would meet him in Silverton to sell their land and get Nizhoni back. He'd sent the bulk of his gunmen there after receiving news from Chief Lonewolf of their agreement. This was good news for the American Cowboys. They would not be facing the bulk of the Baron's gunmen in the rescue attempt. Finally, they gave the news that John wanted to hear. The Baron's train would roll into Durango in two days.

When the Navajo finished their report, Two-Rivers went to John and said, "You are the leader here. May we speak?"

"Yes. What is troubling you?"

"I cannot help any further because of the risk to my people," Two-Rivers said. "But please protect Nizhoni. She is to be my wife."

"We will do our best," John said. "You have our word."

"Your word is valuable to me. Chief Lonewolf speaks good things of you."

"He is a good man. I am thankful to know him."

Two-Rivers nodded to him, then went to his horse and mounted it. The rest of the Navajo did the same, and they began their journey back to their village.

The Cowboys then completed their plan. Because of his knowledge of the terrain and his skill as a horse rider, Ben took the lead in planning how they would board the train. He told them they should launch a surprise attack and ambush the Baron's men like an Apache by boarding through the sides of the train.

Nizhoni would be on a train from Alamosa to Durango, and it passed through the San Juan extension. However, rescuing her during this leg of the ride was too risky because of the treacherous terrain, so they had to wait for the train to reach Durango. Ben stressed the dangers they would face if the train reached the Silverton Pass. The altitude at Durango was 6,500 feet and climbed to 9,300 feet in Silverton. "If we don't board the train before the Silverton Pass, the horses won't make that climb. We must know exactly how the train will enter and leave the Durango station. We will discuss the terrain between Durango and the Silverton Pass in case we need to implement our backup plan." Ben started laying out where the Cowboys would ride and what to expect.

The train route to Durango came out of the mountain bluffs from Chama. The drop was significant for the train, so the speed would be a little faster. Then, the terrain leveled out from the bluffs before crossing the Animas River. The train would then slowly roll into Durango, exchange passengers, get coal, and head north for Silverton. One Cowboy would need to be a passenger and board the train in Durango. They thought Oscar was perfect for this, as he was unknown to Dane or the Baron. Oscar would stay in the train car next to the Baron's and wait for backup. The rest of the Cowboys would then attempt the rescue when the train pulled out of Durango. If that did not work, they would have a second chance at boarding the train at a position two miles before the Silverton

Pass. This area was flat and provided more coverage from large trees. The train would have thirteen cars, including the engine, and the Baron would be in the third car because he liked to be close to the engine in case anything went wrong. Nizhoni would be in the eighth car and away from any passengers, a location that was easier to keep her out of sight to avoid suspicion from others. The Baron did not want any witnesses that he had her in his possession. Two Cowboys would board the left side of the train in the fifth car, and the other two would board the eleventh car on the right side of the train. Once the Cowboys boarded the train, they would systematically work their way toward the eighth car to get Nizhoni. She would be the priority. Only after her safety was ensured would they look for Dane.

The Cowboys agreed that Dane must face justice; otherwise, more people would suffer at his hands. Getting to him would be difficult because only two Cowboys could make their way from the eighth train car to the third train car, where Dane would be with the Baron. Oscar would be near there, in train car four, and would assist with taking care of Dane. The other two Cowboys would take Nizhoni to the caboose for safety. John did not want to split the Cowboys up, but they did not have any other choice.

"One last thing, Cowboys," John said. "Be mindful of other passengers on the train. We don't want to jeopardize bystanders. Ben and Boyd will check the train's passengers once we secure the train."

The Cowboys agreed to the plan and were about to turn in for the night when Frank spoke up.

"Fellas, I want to stress that I'm the only one who will kill Dane. He took my boy. And I will be the man who avenges him."

The Cowboys nodded in agreement, all except for Oscar, who also wanted to kill Dane. But Frank didn't notice this, or he would have spoken with the young Cowboy. Michael was Oscar's best friend, and he wanted revenge as well. He vowed that if he had the opportunity on the train, he would kill Dane regardless of what Frank wanted.

While the rest of the Cowboys slept, Ben found it hard to do so. He wasn't nervous about the rescue—it was because of where he was. He was back in Apache land, back where he was raised, and he felt a sense of fulfillment. Being out in nature was what he had remembered as a child, with his people freely roaming the land. This was where he belonged. He vowed never to leave it again after this rescue.

Nineteen

Alamosa Departure

Dane and the Baron reached the Alamosa train station right on schedule. Their men started loading the luggage on the train that would take them to Silverton. The Baron's northern home was in Silverton, and most of his men were waiting there to execute the Baron's devious plan he had in store for the Navajo. He had received news from the Navajo that they would come to sign his agreement selling their land. They would be prepared. His foreman in Silverton, Lomax, was getting everything arranged for their arrival. A smaller group of his men would stay behind in Alamosa to keep the townspeople in line. He was bringing a handful of his men along on the train ride for protection. Nizhoni, the most important cargo, was already on the train.

"The train is loaded, boss," Dane said with a snarl.

"Good. The sooner we get moving, the better. I don't trust being still."

The steam train wasn't the fastest, but it was efficient. It ran through high-terrain areas that were invulnerable to attacks. The Baron trusted this route more than any other.

Finally, the train left the Alamosa train depot. There were only a few passengers on the train, as the Baron had purchased most of the tickets for his men. The random passengers would be seated in train car five. This also limited the number of potential witnesses. The scenery along the route was beautiful. From the tall sand dunes to the mountains and the trees, the scenery was perfect for Colorado. The Baron's primary home was in Alamosa, and the town was all his—he had hand-picked the sheriff and the US marshal to ensure that he had the lawmen's backing. He used fear and intimidation by his hired gunmen to maintain control of the town. The Baron used that standing amongst the townspeople to take as much money as he could from them. He did so by making 25 cents on every dollar spent from his tax. The townspeople were told that the tax was for their protection. The locals didn't like this, but they had no choice but to go along with the Baron's taxes. If they did not pay, then they could expect a visit from Dane. He wouldn't just beat them but would also harm their women. Some of the children of the business owners who rejected the Baron's taxes had even disappeared.

Nizhoni was trapped in a nightmare. She had witnessed her people being ruthlessly murdered by Dane and his gunmen for no reason. They had taken her from her home, beaten her, and forced her into this dirty train car usually reserved for animals. All she could think about was her people who had been killed by these monsters and returning to her land. She worried that her time in this life was about to end. Her father had always told her to turn to the spirits for guidance in times of need. Knowing this was her only hope, she asked for help from the spirits, and she saw a vision. A vision of her people and her land. From Mount Taylor in the south to Mount Hesperus in the north, the land was as beautiful as the Navajo people were strong. This vision gave her peace and joy. She thanked the spirits for giving her hope. She felt that Mount

Hesperus since it was the last thing she saw in the vision, was close to her.

Little did she know her train was heading for Durango, the home of Mount Hesperus.

Dane and the Baron were settled in the third train car, which was near the engine. The Baron felt safer close to the engine because if trouble arose further back on the train, they could easily detach from the other cars. This was dangerous for the train cars left behind but provided a safety net for a getaway for the Baron if needed. There were ten gunmen, including Dane, on the train. Dane had placed them, armed with Winchester rifles, throughout the train, and he had instructed them to focus on the front and rear of the train, as the Baron felt the cliffs and trees would deter any attacks from the sides. Three gunmen were in the train car with the Baron.

Dane and the Baron discussed how they would expand the railway once the US Cavalry moved the Indians. The Rio Grande Railway would pale in comparison to the Baron's planned construction of a new railway through the New Mexico Territory and Colorado. It would connect to the other railways going north and south, which could make them fortunes to last three lifetimes.

The plan had gone well so far, and they were close to completing it. It was important for there to be no loose ends.

And that was what Nizhoni had become—she could become the witness who blew up their lie about why the Navajo attacked the Baron.

Regardless of what happened, Nizhoni, they both agreed, must die in Silverton.

Twenty

The Rock

Not being allowed to save the woman he loved was not sitting well with Two-Rivers.

He does not trust the Cowboys that Chief Lonewolf had sent. Navajo do not give trust to outsiders so easily. He could not make sense of why, even with the recent unpleasant history of settlers, their respected Chief had approved this mission. Many Navajo in the village were upset with this plan. The elders of the tribe had met recently and agreed to go down the path Chief Lonewolf had set them on. The decision was not popular with the tribe, especially with the younger men. They brought their concerns to a man they hoped could sway the Chief's opinion to allow a war party to assemble to rescue Nizhoni and avenge the tribe by killing her captors. That man was Two-Rivers. He agreed and would speak with Chief Lonewolf.

Chief Lonewolf was walking through the Navajo village. He hoped being out amongst the people could help ease the anxiety he had over Nizhoni. At first, he felt at ease seeing his people. That soon changed when he noticed the unfriendly reception he received. He knew two things were certain for a leader: making hard decisions and having to live with those decisions. No one more than him struggled to control the anger felt toward the murderous bandits that took Nizhoni. His daughter had been abducted, and his people had been killed. He knew the wrong reaction could be the end of the Navajo on their land. Patience would have to become his friend; understanding would have to be his people's blanket. The young Navajo men caused concern for the Chief. Word had spread to the Chief that they were displeased with his decision. Only time would teach them the value of following their elder's choices. They needed to learn that the survival of the tribe was their priority to ensure they did not suffer a fate that would be unrecoverable—the loss of their land.

Chief Lonewolf noticed Two-Rivers walking toward him. This, he thought, would be about the concerns of the young men. It was common in a dispute amongst the tribe to identify someone to approach the elders. Two-Rivers was their peer and their choice. A wise decision indeed thought the Chief.

"Chief, I would like to discuss an issue with you."

"Yes, Two-Rivers, what is troubling you?" He played coy with the young Navajo. Young people need a chance to express their thoughts, not be told those of others. This helped them become better leaders in the future.

"We should not trust these cowboys to save Nizhoni. They do not differ from others we have faced."

"John Rose and his men have earned their place here. What is your grievance with them?"

"They are not Navajo. There does not need to be more than that."

"What would you have me do, Two-Rivers? Do you know a better way for the Navajo?" Chief Lonewolf asked, even though he knew what his answer would be.

"Yes, we need to form a war party. Then go rescue Nizhoni and take vengeance on those killers who have her."

That is what he expected to hear from the young Navajo. They had been building up this thought since the attack happened. The elder's attempt to calm the young men with reason was not working. He felt disappointed when Two-Rivers quickly joined this sentiment. Two-Rivers loved Nizhoni, but he needed to learn to put the Navajo first if he expected to be their leader one day.

"What about the consequences of these actions? What happens when the soldiers return?"

"We will fight, we will win. This is the Navajo way."

Reflecting on the best way to respond, he thought of Winged Rock. The young Navajo needed the spirits to make sense of this issue. He needed an understanding of why this land was so important to the Navajo. The Rock could teach him that. Then he would be the one to convince the other young Navajo that the Cowboys were the only option to rescue Nizhoni.

"Let us talk more. Come on a ride with me."

"Where will we ride?"

"Totah. We need to visit the spirits for guidance."

Two-Rivers was impatient and wanted a resolution now. But he also knew he would have to ride with the Chief to get an answer.

"Yes. I will ride with you. But a resolution needs to be made at sunset."

Chief Lonewolf nodded his head in agreement. The men went to prepare for their short ride to Totah.

Totah, meaning between the waters, was on the Colorado plateau. Three rivers passed through this area, giving it its name. When traveling through the trees of the forest, they would open up on the high desert, exposing the red rock landscape of the Navajo Nation. The scenery made the Navajo people proud. This was their home. Nothing else could compare. The Navajo came to appreciate

it more when they almost lost it following the Navajo Wars. Chief
Lonewolf hoped bringing Two-Rivers to this area would speak to
the young warrior. Protecting their land outweighed anything else
for the Navajo. Even rescuing Nizhoni.

Seeing the red rock landscape, Two-Rivers was filled with a
sense of admiration as he passed through the trees. He had only
been to Totah once before as a child. Pride overcame him, knowing
this was Navajo land.

"Our land is grand. Full of color and wonder." Chief Lonewolf
said.

Still in awe of the scenery in front of him, Two-Rivers only
nodded his head in agreement.

"Let us ride to Totah and find a place to enjoy the sunset."

"Yes. That will be nice." Two-Rivers finally responded.

They rode their horses to an acceptable position. Dismounting,
they found a place to sit. In the distance, they could see Winged
Rock. Quietly sitting, they watched as the setting sun lit up Winged
Rock. The beauty of the scenery was enhanced by the setting sun.

"Do you know the story of Tse Bit a i?" Chief Lonewolf asks.

"Only stories of the Rock and that it brought us here."

"There is more to the story. White men named it Shiprock. To
them, it only looks like an object from the sea. It's so much more to
us. Let me tell you."

Two-Rivers nodded his head in agreement without taking his
eyes off Winged Rock.

"The Navajo were in the lands north of here. The spirits came
to our ancestors and told them it was time to leave that land. Confused, the people asked what would become of them. The spirits
told them their chosen place was ready. The people agreed. They
did not have a way to get to their land. So, the great bird came and
carried them here. Once safely on the ground, the great bird turned

to stone. Winged Rock is the name given to the stone of the bird. The same rock you see before us."

After a brief pause to let the story settle with the young warrior, the Chief said, "The great bird turned to stone because this is our destiny. We stay here on this land and cannot let anything take it away. You and the other young warriors are blinded by hate and revenge. This makes you unable to understand what is at risk for our people. The great bird did not give us this land so that we could lose it by not controlling our emotions."

As Two-Rivers reflected on what Chief Lonewolf had said, the reality of the situation hit him. The Navajo had been in their land for generations. Through that time many had sacrificed to ensure their land was protected. Challenging sacrifices were made by the Navajo. This beautiful land, given to them by the great bird, was bigger than one individual. Even if that individual was the woman he loved, protecting the land must come first. This realization made Two-Rivers emotional. Feeling a great sense of sorrow knowing he could not help Nizhoni brought tears to his eyes. He knew the Chief's plan must be followed. This was a difficult situation for the young warrior to accept, but he had no choice.

"I understand now. I still feel the pain in my heart being ripped out when Nizhoni was taken. How do you make those feelings go away and have patience?"

Pondering this question, the Chief took time to answer. He was distraught over his daughter being taken. He just understood that the Navajo people came before any one person. "Those feelings will never go. That is a burden you carry for those you love. We have to accept whatever outcome is best for our people. This is how we can ensure others will not control us on our land."

With the sun almost completely set, the men got up off the ground and mounted their horses. It was time to return to the village.

"There is one more thing. How can we trust the outsiders sent to rescue Nizhoni?"

"If the Great Bird trusted us to be in the land, how could the Navajo not trust these outsiders? They are helping to protect this land by going on the mission."

The men rode back into the trees and headed east for their village. Two-Rivers knew that going north was the way he wanted to travel.

Durango was to the north, and so was Nizhoni.

Twenty-One

Durango

From the Animas River to the mountain bluffs, it was a sight to see.

You could tell you were in Colorado, with the grandiose mountains and soaring pine trees. Durango was even more surreal, with the Animus River slicing its way through the town. Under normal circumstances, the Cowboys would take this opportunity to rest and fish. But they were here for business. Soon, they would have to board the Baron's train. That the last time they attempted a train rescue they had lost Michael was heavy on everyone's mind as they crossed the river. The river, with its strong currents, could be brutal if you crossed it in the wrong place. The Cowboys picked a safe place to cross and headed to town.

Durango was a small mining town with around 2,000 people. To reach Silverton, Colorado, the builders created a route for the D&RG Railway through the town. This was also done to transport minerals and goods from southern Colorado up north. The Durango smelter was the primary source of its economy, producing silver, lead, gold, and copper. The economy thus prospered, and so did the town.

The D&RG Railway, also called the Rio Grande, was the leading mountain railway company in the United States. It got its nickname "Through the Rockies" because it carved its way through mountains and canyons. This made the D&RG Railway ideal for Durango's terrain. It was the largest narrow-gauge railway network in America, something the Baron hoped to copy with his planned railway. The D&RG Railway had become the best by expanding and building through mountains to transport expensive minerals. The Baron envied this business setup and planned to take some of their business from them with his railway. If the associates knew what he was planning, they would try to stop him. However, he had so far avoided any suspicions from them.

The Cowboys made it to Durango and went to investigate the train station. They needed to find a stakeout location around the station. Based on the information from the Navajo scouts, the Baron's train would roll in at noon. A worker for the railway had told Boyd that the train was light and carrying only twenty passengers, which meant that, not counting Nizhoni, only six innocent passengers would be on the train, all seated in train car five. The plan was to break into groups of two, with John and Frank on the east side of the train station and Boyd and Ben on the west side. Oscar would board the train as a passenger. The other four would then use Ben's plan, using Apache tactics to ambush the train. Once the train pulled out of the station, they would start the rescue operation.

John and Frank situated themselves in the saloon directly past the station, while Boyd and Ben situated themselves at the hotel across from the saloon. This, they believed, was the best angle for the ambush.

Now that they were in position, Oscar headed to the station. On his way to the ticket booth, he heard the train coming. This was the moment he had been waiting for ever since Dane killed Michael. Though Frank had made everyone promise only he should kill Dane, Oscar knew he would take the first chance he got to kill Dane. With every step, his hatred for Dane grew. Michael wasn't just his best friend—he was like his brother.

As the train rolled into its scheduled stop in Durango, Dane and the Baron were discussing the expansion plans for their railway.

"I think we should run our tracks from Ruidoso through Denver. Forget these narrow-gauge tracks," Dane said. He was not a fan of the narrow-gauge railroads and felt they were short-sighted. "The big money is on passenger trains and cargo trains that can't run through narrow-gauge railways. Let's go for the long-term investment," Dane added.

"The short-term investment in these narrow-gauge railways is what will carry us to the long term," the Baron replied. "We need the minerals from the narrow-gauge railway to fund a standard gauge track. We will make it to Denver, but first, we start in the Rockies." The Baron would not be distracted from his vision by Dane, whom he viewed as a vagrant more than anything. But the Baron knew he needed Dane to get to where he was going. Once he was done with him, he would have him put away. But he had to be careful not to let Dane know his actual feelings about him—if he did, then Dane would kill him.

Dane continued to stare at the map as the train came to a stop at the station. "Well, either way, you know my deal. I get my percentage, but I think it would be more by avoiding these trashy mining towns." Dane despised miners and mining towns, preferring to be as far as possible from them. When he looked out the window, he saw Oscar coming from the ticket office and heading to the train platform. Dane knew that Oscar rode with the American Cowboys.

Dane had seen Oscar with the American Cowboys during the El Paso rescue attempt. The Cowboys thought Dane didn't know Oscar, hoping that he would go unnoticed. This was not the case. He quickly started looking out all the windows. Looking for the rest of them.

Oscar showed his ticket to the conductor and boarded. Following the plan the Cowboys had devised, he went into train car number four and found a seat in the back so that he could have eyes on the doors leading to train car three. Now, all he had to do was wait for the signal from the Cowboys that it was time for the ambush.

With every passing minute, he grew more determined to go find Dane and kill him. Frank would be mad, but he was prepared to live with the consequences—just like Frank, he felt he had every right to kill Dane.

***

John and Frank patiently waited for the train to depart so they could give Oscar the signal. Retribution was within his grasp, Frank knew, and he became silent and focused. He was about to bring the man who killed his son to justice.

"How are you holding up, partner?"

Frank did not respond, and they both sat, occupying that awkward pause.

"I'm not doing well. This is the darkest time of my life. Even when I was a slave, I always had hope of freedom. Then, after Maybelle died, I had hope for the future because of Michael. But now, I have no hope, and that has broken me. I just want to kill Dane and bring peace to Michael. I'm not living with hope anymore, just vengeance, and nothing I've done in this life will match the importance of this moment."

John hoped Frank wouldn't let his anger overcome his judgment. He did not want to lose any more Cowboys in a rescue. He also wanted to bring Dane to justice, but he had found his way to honor Michael by naming his child after him.

"Frank, before things get crazy, I need to tell you something. Jane and I decided that we're going to name our baby Michael."

Frank loosened up a little and became emotional. "That is a grand gesture. Thank you, my friend. My son would be proud."

John nodded and patted him on the back, and the both of them resumed their wait. Frank noticed a tear rolling down his cheek. For the first time since Dane had killed Michael, he couldn't hold back his emotions, and he sobbed. He felt John's hand on his shoulder. John quoted Isaiah 33:2: *"Lord, be gracious to us; we long for you. Be our strength every morning, our salvation in time of distress."*

Frank placed his hand on John's, which was still on his shoulder. "Thank you, friend." He was glad to hear God's words this time, but he wasn't ready to forgive. Today was for justice.

The men started to regroup and prepare for the ambush.

***

Dane began looking for Oscar on the train. Was he alone, or was he with the Cowboys, Dane wondered. He had heard that the American Cowboys had broken up. Also, since he didn't think the Navajo would turn to outsiders to help save Nizhoni, he didn't worry about him being a hired assassin—this, then, had to be a revenge mission. Neither Dane nor his men could spot any of the other American Cowboys around the train station. Dane knew he had to find Oscar and kill him. So, he ordered a gunman to guard the Baron and then started looking for Oscar. He took the other two gunmen and went into the adjoining train car. He quickly spotted Oscar sitting in the back. There was a bar in this train car, and Dane, seeing a woman having a drink, got an idea.

The train pulled out of the station, and the Cowboys got ready to ride. Oscar, seeing Dane enter his train car, became tense with anger. Dane slowly walked over to the bar. There was a pretty woman with blonde hair standing at the bar, having a drink. Dane went up to her and started a conversation that appeared to be one-sided, with Dane doing most of the talking.

Dane's back was turned to Oscar, and he seemed completely distracted. Oscar realized he could shoot him right now and have his revenge. But shooting from where he was sitting was too risky —the woman was in his way, and he could end up killing her. This was his chance to make his move and take out Dane, but he had to get closer. If Dane was dead, it would be easier to find Nizhoni, Oscar realized. He would have to use his knife to kill the bandit. To do that, he would have to get next to him while leaving his rifle in his seat. It would be suspicious to approach him with a rifle while inside a train car. He rested his rifle against the seat, then quietly left his seat and walked toward the bar, his eyes locked on Dane. He was almost ready to pull his knife out when a gunman entered the car with a rifle, with his eyes set on Oscar, and walked to the right side of the bar.

Oscar paused for a moment and then kept going. He was all in now. Then, another gunman entered with a rifle, his eyes also focused on Oscar, positioning himself on the left side of the bar.

"You didn't think some Mexican could kill me, did you, kid?" Dane said.

Oscar realized he was in trouble. He had walked into a trap.

Dane spun around, his trademark scattergun pointed right at Oscar, and gave him his infamous wink.

As the train left the station, a gunshot from inside the train startled the Cowboys.

The train car door opened on car four, and Dane stood there with Oscar's lifeless body. He threw the body on the track. The Baron's gunmen would turn the place into a shooting gallery if the

Cowboys moved now and revealed themselves, so they had to hold their positions until the train was out of sight.

As the train left the station, the townspeople rushed over to the lifeless body on the track. The Cowboys, now clear of being spotted by any gunmen, rode over to Oscar's body. He had a shotgun blast on his chest, and they immediately knew it was from Dane's scattergun.

Dane had killed another American Cowboy.

Seeing Michael's best friend lying dead on the tracks caused the fury inside Frank to grow.

"They are getting away. If they make it to the Silverton Pass, we'll never catch them," Ben said, while John pulled Oscar off the rails and placed a blanket over him.

"There is nowhere for them to go but straight to Hell," Frank said and got on his horse. "American Cowboys, let's ride!"

Twenty-Two

Rainstorm

Jane loved being at the ranch. Of course, she loved it more when John was with her. She took great pride in what they had built together. Now they were adding a baby to the family. Though Jane was happy being pregnant, it made doing work around the ranch difficult. Thankfully, Teresa, an excellent horse rider, had quickly made it to the ranch to help her.

Teresa loved this area, and she happily took a break from being in Dulce. She had been through some rough times recently and needed to speak with John and Jane. She just didn't know how to broach the topic now. Jane was happy to have the help and appreciated John thinking of her on his way to Durango with the American Cowboys. She had become friends with Teresa on their trips to Dulce to get supplies at the trading post. Teresa's mom had recently been sick, and she was helping Cade more at the trading post to help cover the doctor's bills. But her mom did not like the hard work at the trading post or the type of men the post brought in. She was a single woman in her early thirties who had spent most of her life taking care of her sick father. Her father had passed away five years ago, and now it was just her and her mom. Teresa and Jane communicated through the letters they exchanged occasionally through the postman. Jane was happy to have her at the ranch because it helped her take her mind off John being gone.

Jane had told Teresa about her pregnancy through their correspondence, and this was the first time they had seen each other after Jane had shared the news.

"Are you ready for lunch, Jane?" Teresa asked.

"Lunch would be good. I could use a little rest. I'm just thankful you're here, Teresa. Thank you for helping."

"It's my pleasure, Jane," Teresa said. "This is better than being at the trading post."

They went inside, and Jane sat down with Teresa as they prepared to eat.

"I'm so happy John and I are expecting," Jane said, tears falling from her eyes.

"Oh, Jane. I'm so happy for you both," Teresa replied. They hugged each other. "You'll be the best mom, Jane. I just know it."

"Thank you, Teresa. We are so happy and thankful for this wonderful gift. God has been so good to us. I just hope John isn't away from me for too long, because I'm going to need help around here." Jane replied.

While they ate their lunch, Teresa mustered the courage to talk to Jane about the situation she was in.

Teresa knew that Jane would understand her problem, but she worried about how she would respond. But now that Jane had said she needed help around the ranch, this seemed like a good time.

"It's funny you mention needing help and us talking about mommas. Because my mom just passed, Jane and I have nowhere to go." Teresa paused, overwhelmed with grief. Her momma meant everything to her, and now she was gone. Teresa had dedicated her life to helping her parents, who had been slaves in Georgia and had suffered so much. After they were freed, they headed for the mountains of the West, where there were no plantations or unpleasant history, seeking a fresh start, and Teresa had tried to help them enjoy this new life.

Jane hugged Teresa while she wept. "Teresa, you always have a place here. Our home is your home."

They continued to embrace each other and cry.

Teresa finally said, "Thank you, Jane, you are a great friend."

After they finished their lunch, they began cleaning the kitchen and, as they were finishing, it began to rain. Jane loved sitting on their porch and watching the rainstorms go through the mountains. She invited Teresa to join her, and they went outside to sit on the porch and enjoy the rain. This was Jane's happy place. From here, she could look at their ranch, which they had built with their hard work, and, as the rain nourished the land, revel in the wonders of God. Jane was proud of their land and the home they had made. Her thoughts went to John and the rescue mission he was on. Every time he left for a rescue mission, she knew that he might not return. She wished he was home, sitting on the porch with her, his arm around her, enjoying one another in the ranch's peacefulness. She prayed every day for his safety and his return home. All she wanted was her American Cowboy.

Twenty-Three

Animas Crossing

Dane entered the third train car with a wide grin on his face. Killing brought him great joy.

"We killed a Cowboy," he said to the Baron with a certain satisfaction. "He was one of John Rose's men."

"Were the others with him?" the Baron asked.

"I don't think so. We will be at the pass shortly and will be in the clear."

"Be on the lookout for the others," the Baron said. "It's not common for them to be alone."

Dane ordered one gunman to go to the engine car and the other two to stay in the Baron's car. "Men, be ready for anything until we reach the Silverton Pass," Dane snarled. He was hoping that the Cowboys would show up—he wanted to kill them all.

***

The Cowboys' horses galloped alongside the Animas River, hoping to catch the Baron's train. They were about five miles behind the train and had to run their horses at full speed to catch it before it reached the Silverton Pass. The Cowboys all rode their horses with purposeful focus. Never before in the history of the American Cowboys had a ride meant this much to these men. Their focused determination was fueled by a collective mindset—bringing Dane to justice. The Cowboys were riding through the Colorado landscape on a low crossing next to the Animas River to ensure that they weren't visible to the Baron's men.

While they were racing to catch the train before it made it to the pass, John knew that more Cowboys might die. But he vowed to do whatever it took to ensure their safety. As the Cowboys drew close to the boarding point for the train, he was more determined than ever to succeed.

The Cowboys made it to the boarding point. To follow Ben's backup plan to ambush the train from the sides, two Cowboys—Frank and Ben, the Cowboys had decided—would have to cross under the train bridge to the other side of the tracks. They would then board the eleventh car from the right side of the train. The bridge, which went over a dry ditch where the river had overflowed, would hide them from the Baron's men.

As Frank and Ben crossed, a piece of lumber from the track fell from the bridge overhead and struck Frank's right arm. The impact nearly knocked him off his horse. He was able to steady himself, but his right arm was broken near the wrist.

They made it to the other side of the tracks and continued their pursuit. His right arm broken, Frank knew it would be difficult for him to board the train, let alone shoot with his Peacemaker.

The Cowboys were successful in getting the jump on the Baron's men: John and Boyd rode their horses close to the left side of the train and boarded the fifth car using the side ladders. John went first, and Boyd followed. The six passengers in the train car were startled by the cowboys boarding their train but calmed when John announced they were the American Cowboys. Now, they had to make their way back to the eighth car, where Nizhoni was. From the other side of the train, Ben jumped onto the eleventh car.

Frank was the last one to board. Using his left arm, he lunged for the side ladder and narrowly grabbed it. He slammed against the car and hit his injured arm, which made him yell.

This caught the attention of a gunman. He immediately started shooting at Frank, who had finally stabilized himself on the side ladder. Ben threw a knife into the gunman's chest, making him fall off the train. Ben went to Frank and pulled him in safely.

"Frank, are you okay? Is your arm hurt?"

"I'm fine. Leave me be. We have a snake to kill."

They now had to make their way to car eight.

John and Boyd, unaware of what was happening to Frank and Ben, heard the gunshots.

"Frank and Ben are getting into it on the other side," Boyd said.

"They are hopefully handling the situation," John replied.

As John and Boyd maneuvered through the sixth car, they stumbled upon a gunman who was scanning the other side of the train to locate Frank and Ben.

"Can you take that gunman out, Boyd?" John asked. "He's a clear shot from your position."

"I will," Boyd replied, then shot the gunman with his Winchester.

"Great shot! Let's keep looking for Nizhoni."

Reaching the seventh car, they saw two gunmen inside, who quickly began shooting at them.

"Get down, Boyd! Two gunmen at 10 o'clock and 2 o'clock!"

They dove for cover behind the wall of the car.

"You take the 10, and I will get the 2," Boyd said.

After a shootout, Boyd managed to shoot his gunman, and John managed to finish the other gunman as well.

Now they were one car away from Nizhoni.

"Good shooting," John said. "Keep your eyes open for Dane. He is around here somewhere."

Boyd nodded his head as they approached Nizhoni's train car.

Frank, since he was tying up his broken right arm with a makeshift sling, was a little behind Ben when he entered car ten. Once inside, a gunman jumped on Ben and they got into a knife fight. Frank tried to rush to help—but he was stopped by another gunman who entered the car. Frank took cover and engaged in a shootout with the gunman. He had to trust Ben to take care of himself. Since Frank was right-handed, he was not very accurate with his left, and reloading was difficult. Because the shooter had Frank pinned down, he did not have a good shot at him.

The gunman Ben was fighting, though strong, was growing tired fast. He was proving to be no match for the young Apache, and soon, Ben got the better of him and subdued him just when Frank also shot the other gunman after he exposed himself trying to shoot Ben. He then helped Frank up, and they moved into the ninth car, where there were no gunmen. They quickly passed it and entered the eighth one, where Nizhoni was supposed to be. The train car was dark and had a musky smell, like animals had been in there. The Cowboys tried to adjust their eyes but were not having much success due to the darkness.

"Nizhoni, are you in here? Your father has sent us," Ben said.

They lit a gas lantern.

As the light slowly filled the train car, they saw a young Navajo woman chained to a pole. It was Nizhoni. "Yes, I am here," she said, weakly. There was a chain attached to her wrist that was locked onto a pole.

"Ben, cover Nizhoni while I get this lock off," Frank said. Ben did so and shielded her face.

Frank shot the chain lock and freed her from the pole. They were about to move her to the caboose when Boyd and John entered the car.

John's relief at seeing Nizhoni safe was short-lived when he noticed Frank's injury. After Oscar's death, he had prayed that no more Cowboys would get hurt.

"Frank, are you okay?" John asked.

"Just broke my arm on the ride. I will be okay."

"Since you're hurt, take Nizhoni to the caboose with Ben and protect her," John said.

"I am no babysitter, John. I am here for Dane, and no one will deny me my vengeance."

"Do not let your thirst for avenging Michael's death jeopardize the safety of the team, Frank," John said.

After a few moments, Boyd said, "Guys, I will stay with Ben and Nizhoni. Frank, go get Dane. It is your destiny."

Frank nodded to Boyd and left with John.

"Frank, I love you, brother. I just want what is best for the Cowboys and yourself."

"I understand. I always put the team first. I can hold my own."

As Boyd and Ben took Nizhoni to the caboose, Boyd saw the last gunman on the roof of the caboose, squatting behind an air inlet.

"Ben, can you get that gunman on the roof?" Boyd asked.

Ben nodded and slipped to the ladder of the caboose that went to the roof. He positioned himself behind the gunman and threw a knife into his back.

The gunman fell off the roof.

Nizhoni was now safely secured in the caboose. "Stay with Nizhoni and protect her," Boyd told Ben. "I need to go help the other Cowboys." He then went off to find Frank and John. He wanted redemption.

John and Frank quickly maneuvered their way to the fifth train car, where the six passengers had now taken shelter under the booths. John again reassured them who they were and that they would be okay. They then left the train car and entered train car four, next to the Barons. Inside, they were immediately infuriated when they saw Oscar's blood on the ground where Dane had shot him. Their resolve—that they would ensure that Dane never hurt anyone again—grew by the second.

Once they approached the third car, they saw the Baron through the small windows.

"There is the Baron. We can get the drop on him here, nice and easy," Frank said.

But as they attempted to sneak closer to the car, a gunman emerged and tried to draw his gun. Frank shot him, and the gunman fell off the train.

"Surprise is not an option now. Let's end this," John said, and they burst into the car and took their positions. Frank went left, and John went right.

Dane and another gunman were near the door entrance that the Cowboys came through.

Frank and Dane's eyes met. Both of them were desperate to finally settle the bad blood between them, and now they had their chance.

"Your time is over, Dane. Prepare to be sent straight to Hell," Frank said.

"How is Michael doing, Frank? Oh yeah, I killed him," Dane replied.

Frank was overcome with so much rage that he no longer felt the pain of his broken arm.

Dane and the gunman rushed toward the Cowboys and engaged in a hand-to-hand fight. Dane took on Frank, and John fought the other gunman.

Meanwhile, the Baron, who had been cowering at the back of the train car, left through the train car door and went to the train engine. He ordered the engineer to detach the engine from the other cars and the gunman to shoot anyone who tried to get into the engine car.

The fight between the men was brutal. Each man was fighting for their life. John, a skilled fighter, was getting the best of the gunman. Though Frank was fighting with a broken arm, he was holding his own against Dane.

Noticing Frank's injured arm, he began targeting it. "Frankie boy, it's only a matter of time before you die. Any last words?" Dane said.

"Yes. How does it feel to be beaten by me twice?"

Dane winked at Frank, then slugged him on his injured wrist, making him yell in pain.

Frank took a big swing at Dane that caught him on the right side of his face.

Realizing that he may lose this fight, a look of worry crossed Dane's face.

"What's the matter, Dane? Are you accepting your fate now?"

Nervous, Dane began looking for a way out of the train car, but he couldn't find one.

John finally knocked the other gunman down, drew his Peacemaker, and shot him with his last bullet. Dane took this opportunity to hit Frank's injured arm again, but he missed as Frank dodged his punch and knocked him to the ground with a massive punch to his face. But on the ground near Dane lay the dead bandit's gun whom John had just shot.

He took it and fired at Frank.

Seeing this, John leaped in front of Frank, causing the bullet from Dane's gun to pierce his chest. Frank caught him, and they fell to the floor.

The engineer, following the Baron's command, removed the pin to disconnect the train engine from the other cars. They were approaching the climb to the Silverton Pass, which would cause the other cars to stop.

The Baron watched the other train cars fall further behind. His plans were ruined, and he was furious. "The American Cowboys will face consequences for this, even if it's the last thing I do," he said.

Dane noticed the cars slowing down and realized that the Baron must have ordered the engineer to separate the cars from the engine. "I can't believe that lousy carpetbagger sold me out," he said.

That he could kill Frank was his only consolation.

"You thought what you did to me at Tupelo wouldn't go unpaid?" Dane said, cocking his gun. "Prepare to meet your son. Tell him I said hello—"

It was then that Boyd, coming from train car four, burst through the door. He shot Dane in the head, who fell to the floor, dead. The evilest man in the West was no more.

Frank looked at Boyd and nodded.

So many times Boyd had felt that he let people down when they needed him. Today he felt redeemed. Then he saw John on the floor.

John's thoughts turned to Jane and his baby. The chance he'd so badly wanted, to be a good daddy, would not happen. The hope he had to grow old with Jane on their ranch was fading. He thought, how could he allow this to happen? So many times, he thought of retiring to their ranch. He could not accept that, too many people needed help. Now who would help his family? He looked up to Frank, and then to Boyd and said, "Please take care of Jane, fellas." Trying to keep their emotions in check, they could only manage to nod their heads to this request. Then John felt his green Bible in his vest. He thought of Romans 14:8, which says: "*Whether we live or whether we die, we are the Lords.*" This gave him comfort, knowing his friends would be there for Jane, and he would be with God.

John, as he was dying, told Frank, "Don't be defined by what Dane did, be defined by your faith in God." He continued, "Jane is going to need help taking care of our baby, and I need you to look out for them. This is your second chance; be the man God has planned for you to be."

"I will be there for them," Frank said, a tear running down his cheek. "You have my word, friend."

John reached into his jacket and took out the green Bible Frank had given to him many years ago. "Don't fight your faith," John said with his last breath. Frank was the person, John knew, that needed to read God's word.

Frank took the Bible. He had been so angry at God for taking Maybelle and Michael, and he had not come to terms with those emotions until he took John's Bible. The fact that he wasn't the one to bring Dane to justice was weighing on Frank's mind. How he could become so consumed with vengeance that he lost sight of who he was made him reflect on this situation. He had comfort knowing that Michael's killer was brought to justice but was saddened by how he had turned his back on what was important to him during these challenging days—his friends and, most importantly, God.

It was time for Frank to turn toward God and appreciate the people he still had in his life.

As the train cars slowed to a stop, he tightly held onto John's green Bible.

Twenty-Four

The Riverbank

The train came to a halt next to the Animas River, and the remaining Cowboys, along with Nazhoni, exited the train. Boyd and Ben carried John's lifeless body. Frank followed behind his friends, unable to help because of his injured arm. Nazhoni followed behind him, still shaken and scared from the ordeal she had been through.

Boyd and Ben laid John's body down on the riverbank, then went back to the train to check on the passengers and ensure there were no gunmen left. Nizhoni, standing behind Frank, was motionless and trying to process everything that had happened so quickly. She couldn't believe she was free. Ben had told her they were the American Cowboys, that John was their leader, and he knew her father, who had sought John's help, and that John had gathered the rest of the Cowboys to rescue her. While she was grateful, she badly wanted to return to her people. But she knew the magnitude of the situation: the leader of the American Cowboys had been killed. This was the time to honor the man so influential in her rescue.

Frank was emotional over the loss of another person he cared about. He slowly walked to John's body and fell to his knees next to his deceased friend. He still held John's green Bible that had been entrusted to him moments earlier. "God, life is already hard enough. Why do you keep taking people away from me?" he said while looking up at the sky. Looking back down at John's body, he laid the green Bible on his chest, covered his face with his hands, and cried. "I cannot take any more loss, Lord. It is too much to bear. Please have mercy on me." He continued to cry momentarily, then removed his hands from his face and stared at his friend's body.

Boyd and Ben finished checking on the passengers and looking for any surviving gunmen. Everything checked out safely, with no gunmen remaining, and the passengers were okay. The Cowboys made their way over to Nazhoni and stood back with her to give Frank time to mourn John. They were also distressed over losing their leader but knew Frank had a special friendship with John. He needed time to grieve.

Frank knew John was a great man. He had never wavered in his friendship from the moment they met at Tupelo until he gave his life to save him. Most white men would not have befriended a colored man from the South. They were always equals, and he even treated Michael as his own. Through all their journeys, he never thought he would be gone. He always believed that a man's true character shows in how he confronts death. In confronting his death, John had proven to be a great man.

As Frank knelt beside his friend's body, a slight wind blew and the green Bible resting on John's chest blew open. Frank, still feeling hopeless over losing so many people close to him, fixed his stare on the pages blowing on top of John. Then the wind stopped blowing and the pages of the Bible settled, and a beautiful multi-colored butterfly landed on the opened pages of the Bible. It had blue wings, with black lines and white spots on the base of its wings. Frank became fixated on the butterfly and lost in its beauty. He then noticed the page of the Bible that the butterfly was resting on; it had handwriting at the top of the page. He slowly reached for the Bible to read the writing on the page, which caused the butterfly to fly away.

The writing was John's and said "Prayer for Frank". Four verses were circled below that from Romans, 5:1-4, which said, *"Therefore since we have been justified by faith, we have peace with God through our Lord Jesus Christ. Through him, we have also obtained access by faith into this grace in which we stand, and we rejoice in hope of the glory of God. Not only that, but we rejoice in our sufferings, knowing that suffering produces endurance, and endurance produces character, and character produces hope."*

Frank was shocked to read this scripture in John's Bible, that he had marked for him. John had become a faithful man and was always telling others about faith. He found it overwhelming to accept that his friend, John, actively sought ways to help him through scripture while he was lost. After losing Michael, Frank became consumed because he had lost all hope and actively sought vengeance, while his dear friend sought wisdom from God's word to help show him that his hope was still alive and well in his relationship with God. How could he have been so shortsighted? The peace he sought was available all along, not through a gun, but rather through his faith in Christ. He hugged that green Bible that he received years ago from Pastor Clerkley, closed his eyes, and thanked God for this gift of grace offered through Him. Frank's suffering had been great and losing Maybelle, Michael, and John would never fade, but he could endure thanks to the hope offered through his relationship with God.

Frank opened his tear-stained eyes and placed a hand on John. "Thank you, my friend. Rest easy until we meet again."

Frank rose to his feet and took in the beauty of the Animas River flowing by and the glorious Colorado mountain scenery. Then, his butterfly friend fluttered up to him momentarily and then flew off behind him. He turned to watch the butterfly as it fluttered before flying away. Frank's eyes settled on Ben and Boyd standing next to Nazhoni. As his eyes filled with tears, he managed a smile toward his friends. The men started walking toward each other and all embraced upon meeting. He was thankful for these men still in his life and vowed the American Cowboys would continue to ride.

The men wept for John. Their leader was gone, but not their vision for protecting others.

Twenty-Five

Homecoming

Chief Lonewolf spent many hours of his days thinking about Nizhoni, and every day his grief grew. Some days he felt hopeless, and he feared that he would never see his daughter again. To distract himself, he often went into the woods on the nearby hills to be at one with the spirits. The walk was helpful; it eased his mind and allowed him to think. He often regretted not spending more time with Nizhoni and not having warriors accompany the women gatherers. His people had questioned his judgment about the deaths of so many Navajo, causing regret and sorrow to pick at him daily, and it wasn't getting easier. What was more, some of the Navajo warriors had complained to him that he shouldn't have brought in outsiders to rescue Nizhoni—after everything they had gone through, his people did not trust outsiders. The Navajo people were not aggressive, but if pushed, they could stand up for themselves. Chief Lonewolf's talk with Two-Rivers at Winged Rock helped to ease some of those concerns. He knew he still had to mend this difficult situation in due time. And since he'd had no news about the mission, he feared that it meant the worst.

The young Navajo boy was running as fast as he could through the Rocky Mountain juniper trees and New Mexico Territory locust bushes to reach Chief Lonewolf, who was on the hilltop nearest to the tribe's village. The smell of the towering ponderosa pines was sweet and strong as the boy made his way up the small hill; every step he took was announced by the crunching of the ponderosa pinecones beneath his feet.

The Chief could hear the young boy's call in the distance. He was standing on the hillside and made his way to the voice.

Once he made it to Chief Lonewolf, the boy took a minute to catch his breath. "Please come to the village. We need you now."

If he was sent to return to the village from the hilltop, it was important, he knew. He mounted his horse, pulled the young boy onto its back, and quickly galloped toward the village. He feared whether this was bad news about Nizhoni. The young boy's silence spoke volumes. He knew he needed to be strong for his people, and he began preparing himself to show strength.

His horse was swift, and the village was soon in sight. He commanded the horse to go even faster. He was desperate to find out what was wrong.

When he arrived at the village, he saw a crowd. They were silent once they saw him approach. Fearing the worst, Chief Lonewolf dismounted his horse, suddenly becoming weak in his knees.

The crowd parted, and in the middle were the American Cowboys, and Nizhoni.

She was alive! The Navajo began chanting and dancing with joy. She ran to her father, and they embraced. He cried and thanked the spirits and whispered to her, "Welcome home, my daughter." Nizhoni couldn't help but sob. She had thought many times that she would never be back in her village with her people. But now she was home and in her father's arms. They continued to embrace, and the Navajo people celebrated around them.

Two-Rivers, who was out hunting, was just returning. Hearing the sounds of celebration, he rode his horse over to see what was happening. Once he saw Nizhoni in the middle of the crowd hugging her father, he got off his horse, ran over to her, and embraced her. They both wept with joy. His beloved had returned safely, and he vowed to never let go of her. Looking at Chief Lonewolf, he nodded his head and smiled. The decision to trust the Cowboys to rescue Nizhoni was the right one. She was safely home, and the threat to the Navajo lands was over. Chief Lonewolf deserved much credit.

Seeing the joy of the Navajo people, Frank, Boyd, and Ben smiled. Nizhoni then told her father about the Cowboys who had been killed, and Chief Lonewolf's smile faded. He knew how great the loss was for the American Cowboys. The loss was huge for all the people of the territory they served. John was known to be a fair man with good intentions, especially for the Navajo people. John, in saving his daughter, had paid the ultimate price. Chief Lonewolf stopped the celebration and called to his people.

He explained to his people what John's sacrifice meant to the Navajo. "He was a good man. He was an outsider, but he sacrificed his life for us, people who are different from him. There's no greater sacrifice in life than to sacrifice yourself for others. His actions, and those of the American Cowboys, will help us stay on our land and prevent another Long Walk." Then, to honor John's sacrifice, he announced a funeral riding party going to his home in Chama.

Frank thanked Chief Lonewolf and the Cowboys prepared to take John home.

Twenty-Six

Return of an American Cowboy

There was a rainstorm coming toward the Rose's ranch.

Jane and Teresa had been working diligently at the ranch, trying to finish their work ahead of the rainstorm. They needed to get more vegetables to prepare for when John and the Cowboys returned. Even with no news about the rescue, she prepared for their anticipated arrival. With Durango being close, they should be home any day now. The steady work also helped to ease her mind.

"Jane, riders are coming down the road to the ranch gates," Teresa said.

At first, she was excited. That feeling quickly passed when she noticed there were only three Cowboys and five horses. She knew horses without a rider meant cowboys had died. A thunderclap resounded through the valley.

Jane stood still, praying. "Please let John be okay. Lord, I can't lose him." As a light rain fell, she imagined the worst.

Frank thought the rainstorm was matching the sorrow in his soul as they approached Jane and Teresa.

"This is going to be rough," Boyd said.

"The hardest thing I've ever had to tell someone," Frank replied.

"Do you need us to give her the news with you?" Ben asked.

"No, I need to tell her myself."

He had felt a hole in his heart ever since John died, and he knew it would be even harder on Jane. They were like family and had been through so much. He thought back to his friendship with John and the adventures they had shared. His last words still impacted Frank: "Don't fight your faith." He hadn't opened his Bible since Michael's death; he didn't know how he could keep his faith after losing everything. First Maybelle, then Michael. But the truth hit him after he lost his best friend. He had allowed vengeance to take over his life, causing him to neglect the best parts of his life. "Don't fight your faith." He knew those words would stick with him for the rest of his days. He felt soreness in his right arm, but the swelling from his broken arm had reduced. The Navajo had helped him with the injury so that it could heal correctly. He took the green Bible John gave him out of his vest and placed it into his satchel so that it didn't get wet. He started reading it again after John's death, and he felt renewed by the scripture in Psalm 147:3: *He heals the brokenhearted and binds up their wounds.* He was healing now, and he knew he had to be strong for Jane. Faith in God would allow him to endure.

As the riders got closer, Jane saw they were Frank, Boyd, and Ben. Then the realization hit her: John was gone.

She sobbed, becoming faint. She felt like she might fall. Noticing this, Teresa steadied Jane with her arm around her waist. John was her life, and now he was gone, and processing that thought was unbearable. A wave of sorrow swept through her soul.

Teresa leaned close to Jane and said, "I will be here for you, I promise."

Nodding her head, she wearily replied, "Thank you, Teresa."

Behind the Cowboys, Jane saw Navajo riders filling the skyline. She recognized Chief Lonewolf in the middle. The Navajo people were paying their respects to John. Ben had spoken of this tradition the Indians practiced as a show of respect for deceased warriors. Being her first time seeing this consoled her.

The ride toward the cabin grew harder every moment for Frank. It was important for them to bring John back to his ranch for burial. They had buried Oscar near the Animas River because of his love for Colorado. For John, he needed to be brought home.

As he passed the gates, he knew the American Cowboys would never be the same, but they would continue to ride. Boyd and Ben stopped at the gate to allow Frank space to speak with Jane. They had agreed on the riverbank of the Animas to keep riding together. John's memory and shared ideals to protect people who could not protect themselves would endure.

"Jane is going to need us," Boyd said to Ben.

"Yes. The baby will need guidance. I vowed to never leave my people's land. Being here will help me keep that vow and help John's family."

"Losing John will affect all of us. I think it will bring us closer together," Boyd said.

"We will also need to help Frank through this challenging time. He has suffered many losses," Ben replied as the men watched him continue riding his horse toward Jane.

Frank was grateful for his fellow Cowboys. He needed them now more than ever. Approaching Jane and Teresa, he vowed to always take care of Jane and the baby, as he had promised John. It amazed him the impact John had on so many people—even the Navajo were here out of respect for him. He felt blessed to have known him. He was a good man and a great friend. As he dismounted, Frank asked God for strength.

Tears steadily streamed down Jane's cheeks. She couldn't believe John was gone. How could she live without him? Even breathing did not seem possible without John. Frank walked toward the women, and Jane saw John's body wrapped on top of his horse. The memories they had shared flooded her mind, including their first dance at the Red River Railway Station. Moments they spent together while on the Goodnight–Loving Trail. The night he proposed to her under the Texas stars. Memories she would forever cherish.

As the rain came down on the Rose's ranch, so did their dream of building a family together with John's death. His dream of being a father had ended before he could hold their baby. Never did she dream of raising their child by herself. They had so much time left. Now it was over. She knew she could never love another. Her heart was only for John. She would place what remained of her heart with this new life growing inside her. From this rain would come new life, ever-changing, with a piece of what came before remaining. Likewise, life would continue for Jane with the baby on the way. John may be gone, but a piece of him will always remain with them.

Everything inside her told her to break down and mourn. But she refused and walked toward Frank. She would long for the day when she would meet John again in the heavens. Her star would be racing across the sky to be reunited with him. There would be time to mourn him later. Now was the time to honor John, her American Cowboy, who was finally home.

Twenty-Seven

Epilogue

1891

The Baron stood at the Silverton train station, eagerly awaiting his train heading south to Durango. It has been a long winter with nothing for him to think about except killing the American Cowboys. He knew the Navajo had misled him as well. Their Chief would pay a price for that. The snow has been constant and unrelenting, making the railway south impassable. It was all his men could do just to stay alive. Finally, enough snow melted, with spring in the air, for the train to resume.

"Let's get going, I have waited long enough to kill these Cowboys."

"We will soon boss; vengeance will be yours," replied Lomax.

Lomax was the Baron's ranch foreman in Silverton. He was an older man of sixty with a white beard and hair to match. He had now been forced to take charge of security for his boss since Dane was dead. He privately feared he would have a similar fate if he went south.

"Quit being afeared, you are riding south with me, but only to Durango."

Puzzled by this statement from his boss, Lomax replied, "What do you mean, boss? I thought we were going to get the Cowboys."

"My men that are killers will get them. Coots like you will man the ranch."

Relieved, but also getting irritated, Lomax retorted, "I can handle these American Cowboys. Seems like half of them are dead anyway."

"No, they would kill you; but I have a huckleberry meeting us in Durango that will handle them."

The train was now pulling into the train station, and the Baron turned to Lomax and punched him square in the nose, knocking him to the ground.

"Don't you ever question me again, old man. Next time you die." The Baron demanded retribution for what the American Cowboys had cost him. Violence, he felt, was an act he needed to partake in himself. This is who he would be now. Violence bred through anger would be his motivation. Lomax was the first to experience this.

In his younger days, Lomax would have killed a man for doing this. Nowadays, he knows to be patient. He would go to Durango with the Baron, then head back to Silverton. Then keep on riding north to Denver. He was done working for this carpetbagger.

"Get up and get my bags. I don't want to be here any longer than needed."

Lomax got up, wiping the blood from his nose then grabbing his bags.

"Who's this huckleberry meeting us in Durango, boss?"

Without taking his eyes off the train now coming to a halt he replied, "Jesse Evans from Lincoln County. He has unfinished business with the American Cowboys, just like me."

Lomax tensed up upon hearing that name. Evans and his gang The Boys had terrorized the New Mexico Territory for years. They had stopped after his arrest in Lincoln County at the hands of the American Cowboys. That was only because Evans was in jail. Now he was out and rumored to be back in action. If he was getting involved, Hell was at their door.

"I thought he and The Boys went south for Mexico," Lomax passively said.

"Some of The Boys did, Evans did not. He's been waiting for the right time for revenge."

Lomax was even more convinced that he would part ways with his boss after Durango. He was too old to die working for this scoundrel. The train came to a complete stop, and he carried the Baron's bag aboard.

Before following Lomax onto the train, the Baron looked southward toward Durango. After a long miserable winter, he would soon have a chance for revenge. Through mail correspondence, Evans had told him who they would visit first to get the American Cowboys' location. It would be at a trading post in Dulce. The man's name was Cade. Evans and The Boys would make him talk, then the Cowboys were next. As for Chief Lonewolf, he had something special planned for him.

"Vengeance is coming; you will all beg for death once I get a hold of you."

The Baron climbed onto the train. The man who sent Dane on his killing spree was now out for payback for his devious plan being spoiled. A war was coming for the American Cowboys and their friends, with death following.

Every man would face death. What would make these men was how they faced death.

Acknowledgments

Thank you to my mother Barbara and Uncle Jeff for taking me to New Mexico and Colorado in my youth. Gaylon and Zelda for their love and sacrifice for the family. Don Jennings for his knowledge of the 'Old West' and for teaching me about the Colt Peacemaker. A special acknowledgement to Tauheed Rushdan and Corey Clerkley for inspiring Frank. To my amazing wife Teresa, thank you for always supporting me. Love you.

In Memory

Stephanie Townsend

Jackson Warnick

Corey Clerkley

Other Works By Aaron C. Rhodes

He's My Son: From the Road to Glory

Redeemed: Finding Your Way Back to Glory

Learning to Breathe

Milton Keynes UK
Ingram Content Group UK Ltd.
UKHW010704220524
443011UK00010B/160/J

9 798218 377144